THE
MYTH
OF JUNE

By The Same Author

The Violents

The Myth of June

The Oath of Eve

The Wrath of Raine

Non-Fiction Pen Name

Then I Was Taken by Alaina Davis

THE MYTH OF JUNE

The Violents Book One

A. B. Daniels-Annachi

First published in Australia 2022

This paperback edition 1

Pacific Publications

P.O. Box 441 Norfolk Island NSW 2899

Copyright © 2022 Ariana Daniels-Annachi

Internal design © Pacific Publications/Etheric Designs

Cover design & Artwork © Etheric Tales & Edits

Typeset by ProDesign, Etheric

Edited by Darcy Werkman – The Bearded Book Editor

All rights reserved. No part of this book may be reproduced in any form or by any electronic or mechanical means including photocopying, recording, storage in an information retrieval system, or otherwise – except in the case of brief quotations embodied in critical articles or reviews – without permission in writing from its publisher, Pacific Publications.

The book is a work of fiction. Names, characters, places, and incidents are either a product of the author's imagination or are used ficticiously. Any similarity to real persons, living or dead, business establishments, events, or locales is coincidental and not intended by the author.

Any brand or product names used in this book are trademarks of their respective holders and are not associated with Pacific Publications.

ISBN 978 0 6452383 3 4

To my readers – Welcome to the universe,
I hope you enjoy your stay.

And Poseidon… maybe if you weren't
such a dick, I wouldn't have had to
write this book.

Please read content information
(TW) on www.abdanielsannachi.com
before reading this series.

1

As soon as he'd settled the heaviest storm to take New York in ten years, Typhon wove down through currents of wind. Enjoying the weightlessness of being intertwined with air, he spun a loop before stopping in front of a small house. A white picket fence welcomed him to Leonard Street. He was amazed to see that the flower beds had held through his gales.

He stepped through the gate smoothly and took the stone path up to the leaf-littered porch. He looked down, making sure that he was human-sized and that his suit was in order, before reaching up and rapping on the door. Nothing stirred in the house while he waited. He leaned down and brushed a stray blade of grass from his leather shoes, letting out a light chuckle. He would never understand the fashion of the first decade in any century. Although the eighteen-hundreds had been far worse than this, the fashion that straddled the turn of nineteen-ten was truly atrocious. Some of the other Olympians were lucky they didn't have to come down to Earth.

Typhon straightened and knocked again, shaking himself for getting distracted. He was here on a mission. It was vital he take care of the man that saw him. If he was left to his own devices . . . well, the damage would be unspeakable.

He thought back to the night before. Having a human take notice of him in his godly form was unheard of. He had been doing his best to protect the family he knew must live here. A massive branch nearly six feet long had shaken loose from his spin-up of rain, and when it cut a path through the wind for this man's living room window, Typhon had leaped out of his wind current and raced after it. In turning the branch from its path of potential destruction, time seemed to slow. The man in the house was looking through the window at the time, and his jaw had dropped as they made direct eye contact.

Typhon shuddered. It had been quite unsettling to watch someone notice his face suspended in the air.

Seconds passed before the door swung open wide. "Don't you know it's rude to—" The man's words were cut short as Typhon met his eyes.

"Hello, my name is Ty. I was passing through and thought I'd ask if you could spare a cup of tea."

The man cocked his head slightly, before shaking it hard and dropping his jaw. He blurted out, "I saw you!"

Typhon grimaced, shocked at the outburst. The fact that this man's reaction was so intense was not a good sign. He schooled his features and reached out to place a hand on the man's shoulder, making him flinch.

"It's okay," Typhon murmured.

He let the warmth of summer days seep down through his fingers, and the man instantly relaxed.

The man stepped back and motioned for Typhon to enter. Typhon stood a few inches taller than the man, and he wondered if he should have shrunk down more. He didn't interact with mortals often. As he passed a mirror, he caught a glimpse of his reflection. His hair looked like it was on fire, reflecting colors of an autumn leaf, and his suit looked exactly like one that a bank owner would wear now. He looked at his host in the mirror and noticed him wrinkle his nose and cock his head.

"Something wrong?"

"No, it's just . . . you smell like storm." The man shook his head and held out his hand. "I'm William."

What a strange thing to say. Typhon spun and stretched out his own hand, offering a light squeeze. Electricity crackled between them and William's shoulders relaxed further as Typhon threaded more calm through their touch.

"What can I help you with?" William asked in an unsteady voice.

Typhon gave him a curious look. "You invited me in for tea, remember?"

William shook his head, then seemed to hesitate and nodded instead. Typhon watched him carefully. As much as he was looking forward to a warm drink and the opportunity to observe a human or two, this visit was purely business.

William was the first mortal in centuries to gaze upon him in his godly form, and the last one had gone mad. He hoped this time would be different. Perhaps their minds had become stronger over the years.

Typhon followed him to the kitchen and paused in the doorway, leaning on the frame and crossing his arms. "So, what's been new, friend?"

William busied himself by pulling cups from the cabinet and setting a tea ball in each one.

"Oh, the CEO of the plant stepped down this week. Some woman is taking over. I don't mind terribly, but we all said she'll have her hands full trying to manage such a large team of men. It's uncomfortable how times are changing sometimes. I swear when I was a child, my mother would have been beaten for suggesting going to work.

"Oh! Our baby was born last night! Juniper, we named her." He turned and handed Ty a saucer and teacup, beaming. "She is the cutest. Looks just like her mother, but might have my eyes. We'll have to wait and see if they turn later."

Ty nodded along as William spoke, trying to seem intrigued by the story. He didn't notice anything too strange about William, so perhaps his brain was intact. A baby on the other hand . . . *that* was interesting. Especially one born during one of his storms. He hadn't seen a baby in ages!

Typhon interrupted William's rambling to ask, "May I see her?"

The new father nodded quickly and set his cup down, nearly running down the hall. Typhon reached out a strand of his calming energy to make sure William didn't worry. He wasn't going to harm them in any way.

He waited quietly and sipped his tea, looking around the kitchen and smiling as he took in the modern decorations. The house was small, but it felt cozy.

William reappeared after a moment and cleared his throat. Typhon whirled and a grin broke out across his face as his eyes fell on the bundle in William's hands. He carefully set his drink down to examine the baby. She looked like most infants, with nothing obviously special about her. But maybe she would be different when she grew.

Looking at her puffy pink cheeks and pouting mouth, Typhon smiled.

"It's not often that the gods came down and have the chance to bless a mortal child, you know, but this one must be something special. Especially considering that your mind seems to be intact." He looked up at William, who looked confused. "Surely, no harm would come from leaving her with a gift. But what gift could fit such a child?"

William leaned against the counter and, with a careless movement of his arm, Typhon's teacup crashed to the floor, shattering loudly and sending splinters of glass flying up. A small sliver of porcelain shot through the air, and Typhon whipped out a hand, balancing June in the other, and caught the chunk just before it scraped the baby's cheek.

He cleared his throat and glanced at the new father again, who had shock written on his face, before announcing, "I, Typhon, Titan God of Wind and Storm, bless this child with protection." He smiled. "I'll always be around to make sure she's safe."

William nodded as if he understood the importance of that statement, while Typhon watched him. William's hands trembled as he held his arms out to take Juniper back. Typhon couldn't be sure, but it felt as if a bit of the new father's essence cracked then, wavering the air of calm wrapped around them both.

18
Years Later

2

June stood behind the counter at Mr. Denny's diner, staring at the blank wall next to the door. The white paint was chipping, revealing drab cinder block beneath it. She wondered when the last time this place had been renovated. Sighing, she turned her attention to the order pad in front of her. The pen in her hand had been poised to write table three's order, but she had been too busy daydreaming about battles between gods to realize that Chef was still waiting for the ticket. She quickly scribbled their order down and tore the sheet from the pad. Turning around, she sighed again as she shoved it under the clip above the kitchen window.

"Cheeseburger, chicken sandwich, and fry for three!" she called through the window.

Chef grunted from across the kitchen, and she went back to the register. Resting her arm on the counter and leaning down to scribble on the notepad, she wrinkled her nose in disgust.

No matter how many times she scrubbed the countertop, it was always sticky.

The air in the restaurant was hot, laden with the smell of burnt grease and salt, and the collar of her uniform scratched her neck. She pulled at it, and then reached to straighten her skirt, her mind wandering back to the gods. She wondered if Athena's battle skirt was as uncomfortable as her own, or if Artemis could move as swiftly as normal if she were to wear this gods-forsaken dress. June began to doodle in the corner of the pad, sketching the outline of an ax. How she wished something exciting would happen. She wasn't sure why she was so obsessed with the gods. They weren't all that prevalent anymore, but she'd always felt close to them.

As she drew, her thoughts played to old memories, thinking about her friend Ty and wondering what he was up to. He had been around for her entire life, from the time she could toddle to when she graduated a couple months back. Strange things always happened when he was about. Leaves would swirl in unnatural patterns around her or the wind would suddenly stop when she told him she was cold. She had always imagined he could be a god of some sort, but he never let on if her inklings held any merit.

She became sad as her thoughts turned to the day she walked with her diploma at school. Ty was there, of course—he was always there. He wouldn't miss the chance to celebrate June making it in life with the class of '26. Her mother was also there, but, as usual, her father was nowhere to be found—likely drunk and slumped over at some secret bar. Her mother didn't let on if she knew where he was, but she never did.

Her poor mom, who had her personality beaten down over the years by William, seemed to be a husk of a person now. She had gone through the motions of congratulating June and buying her a slice of pie to celebrate, but June could tell that she wasn't really present the entire night.

June finished her little sketch and smiled at it. As she set the pen to paper to draw something else, the brass bell on the front door chimed, and she looked up to see a man walk in.

He wore a dark-blue suit with thin, white stripes and a white fedora with blue ribbon in the same almost-black shade as the rest of his attire. He took off his hat and hung it on the rack next to the door while she tore off her drawing page and straightened her skirt.

"Hey there!" June called.

The man didn't respond, instead waving his hand nonchalantly and heading to the back of the diner. He slid into an empty booth without looking back.

June sighed and shook her head. Picking up her pad and a menu from the shelf under the register, she made her way to the man's table and set the menu in front of him.

"Can I get you a drink?"

The man ignored her and looked at the menu. She waited for a few seconds before tapping her foot and crossing her arms. One of *those* customers.

"I'll come back in a few minutes then."

He nodded at the table and fiddled with a ring on his left pinky.

Turning away, June rolled her eyes and moved to the kitchen window, where Chef had just placed an order. She carefully balanced the plate of fries on her forearm before grabbing the other two plates. The woman at table three smiled politely as June served them. June had to restrain herself from rolling her eyes again as she remembered Mr. Denny hammering in the importance of always serving the man first. He knew that society had come a long way — after all, if this had been twenty years ago, June wouldn't have been allowed to work — but that didn't stop him from keeping to some of the old traditions. June asked if the couple needed anything else before heading back to the strange man in the suit.

Poised with her pen in hand, she put on her sweetest voice. "Are we ready to order?"

The man looked up at her and smiled, and her heart skipped a beat. He had the most striking eyes she had ever seen, in a shade of blue that could only be found in the ocean. Seafoam bordered his iris, and aegean waves crashed around his pupil. Although he appeared young at a glance, small wrinkles creased around those breathtaking eyes. Twin streaks of silver hair met his temples, and he had the slightest indent in his chin, which accented his strong jawline perfectly. To put it bluntly, this man was handsome.

June realized she was frozen in place and sucked a breath in before smiling back. When the man opened his mouth and spoke, a wave of dizziness came over her.

"Black coffee and a piece of pumpkin pie, please . . . Juniper?"

His coarse voice startled her, as she wasn't expecting the air of authority it commanded. She glanced down at her name tag and laughed. "Oh, yeah, I forgot I was wearing that. I actually go by June. I normally wear one that says 'June,' but I left it at home and this was all I had in my cubby." She realized she was rambling and snapped her mouth shut.

The man's stark white teeth shone as he smiled wider. "I see. Well, it's nice to meet you, June." He dipped his head before continuing. "My name is Don."

A light blush crept into June's cheeks as she gave him a quick curtsy, pulling her skirt out on one side. "Much obliged, Don. I'll fetch your pie and coffee real quick."

"No rush, darlin'. Would you care to join me? It's getting close to dinner."

She fiddled with her pen as she glanced at the clock on the wall. She was due for a break. This might be her only chance to have one before closing in three hours.

"Yeah, I could do that."

Don nodded and turned back to the menu, and June took that as a dismissal. She quickly walked behind the counter, brain feeling fuzzy as she sliced the largest piece of pie that would be allowed and placed it gently on one of the newer dessert plates. She poured a cup of coffee—not half full like Denny insisted she do to save money, but right to the top—and made her way back to Don, careful not to spill a drop.

She ran to fetch her own mug of coffee, mixed with milk and sugar, and returned to slide into the booth opposite her new dinner partner.

The two sat together for nearly an hour, chatting about daily life. June learned that Don was an important businessman that lived just outside the city. He was single, his last name was Whittaker, and she assumed he made a lot of money, based on the fact he wore a nice gold bracelet that matched his ring and had a navy-blue handkerchief in his jacket pocket made of silk. He was in midtown for some business and had to get home quickly. He'd done a lot of traveling all over the world and had too many stories to share and not enough time to tell them to her. June was intrigued. She felt like she could tell him anything.

"So what about your parents, June? I imagine you're living with them until you find a man?" His voice sounded like sandpaper and made her smile.

"No," she replied, spinning her spoon in her mug. "My father isn't the nicest person. I hate to speak ill of him, but my mother says he was completely different before I was born. I hate how he's treated her, and frankly, he scares me. He gambles, which stresses him out, then he drinks, but breaking the law stresses him out, so then he takes it out on my mom." June paused and looked at Don, whose eyes were trained intently on her. "My mom was—is a wonderful woman. When I was a kid, she was full of life and light. She was a gem. I think the years with my father have worn her down. She seems so . . . empty now. I want nothing more than for her to get to be her own person again.

"When I graduated, Denny, who runs this place, offered me a job—and the apartment next door. He only had Chef working here and was tired of waiting tables. Frankly, I think he was just excited to have someone he could pay less than most. So I moved, and now I work."

Don nodded and his half smile pulled out a dimple on his left cheek. The light brush of stubble on his cheek caught the light and made her stomach flip.

She finally decided that he had to be about forty, old enough to be her father but young enough to be as fit as his suit made him look. She was absolutely enthralled, and became even more so when he took the time to ask what she planned to do now that she was out of school.

"I think I'm going to try to get into that new art school." She propped her elbows on the table and clasped her hands under her chin, looking off dreamily. "I love sculpting, and I think I'm pretty good at it. I want to sell my pieces to collectors all over the world. My mom was an artist, although she wouldn't say it. Her paintings made me so happy growing up, and I want to make others happy like that."

June turned her attention back to Don and noticed that he looked anxious. His knee began bouncing under the table and he glanced at his watch.

"Hey, hun, I think I need a smoke. Do you mind if we move this outside? I don't enjoy smoking in the same place I eat."

His voice sent a thrill through her stomach. "Not at all," she squeaked out.

Don smiled. "Lead the way, then."

The pair rose together, and Don held out his hand to let June walk in front of him. She blushed as thoughts about a future with this man crept into her mind. Each step closer to the smoking area behind the diner led her deeper into the daydream of a little house on the river with Don and two young boys playing in the backyard.

When they finally reached the back of the diner, deep in an alleyway, June stopped and looked around, coming back to real life. The alley stunk, and she realized that was because of a massive pile of trash to the side. It was clear there was once a bin under the pile of swollen, rotting food waste and wrappers, but it had long since disappeared. The alley was dark, almost creepy. Where the street in front of the diner was still clear under the dusky sky, this tucked-away corner was more like stepping into midnight.

"Wow, I forgot how dark it was back here. We should really install—"

Her sentence was cut off by a large, calloused hand clamping over her mouth.

Panic rushed through her body, electrocuting each nerve and limb as her mind raced, trying to remember what to do in this type of situation. A broad body pushed against her back and the smell of Don's strong cologne wrapped around her. Her shoulders pressed against his chest, and she realized she was having trouble breathing because his forearm was crushing her ribcage.

"Listen here, darlin'. I don't have much time to go through the nonsense of seduction." His hot breath on her ear made her whimper in fear. His voice, which had previously sounded strong and firm, now sounded terrifying. "I have to hit the road in less than an hour, and you gotta get back to work. So here's what's gonna happen. I'll let go of you, and you're gonna lie down on that little patch of grass there." He motioned to the three square feet of grass that sat off the alley directly behind the diner. Walled on three sides, there was nowhere to run from that spot.

"You're gonna lift that cute little skirt of yours and stay quiet. If you don't, or if you try to scream or run, this'll be incredibly painful for you. Got it?" A tendril of his coffee-tainted breath wrapped around to her nose and tears welled in her eyes as he squeezed her jaw harder. She nodded as well as she could, and he chuckled. "Good." He let go.

The moment June felt the pressure release from her face, she bolted. Two steps down the alley, arms flailing, and mouth open to scream, she was stopped short by Don's huge hands yanking her back. He grabbed her at the waist and spun her around, throwing her to the ground just short of the grass. She tried to scream again, and he shoved a hand on her back while stuffing his silk handkerchief in her mouth before anything more than a muffled squeak could escape.

Don seized her hair in one hand, using the bunch of her tight bun to steer her up onto her knees, before using his other hand to yank up her skirt and tear through her stockings. Braced on all fours, June shivered as the cold air hit her back and made her hair stand on end. Don used a knee to separate her legs, roughly shoving his way between them. Small bits of asphalt dug into June's palms and knees as she tried to support herself. He let go of her hair and reached around to yank her hands up, holding them tightly behind her back with one hand. Her face fell hard onto the ground, where the tiny pebbles underneath them dented into her cheek. Her tears began to flow freely then, adding to the mud already lining the alley. She heard a zipper over her gasping sob and felt Don's body heat move closer before he forced himself inside her. She tried to scream but the silk caught every sound, only letting air escape and meld with the light breeze around them.

As Don had his way with her, her sobs faded and tears stopped falling into the puddle beneath her. The mud stung her eyes and she tried to blink it out, but every forward movement forced more dirt up. She was vaguely aware of how greasy his hands were from her hair gel, before she blacked out the world and let her mind wander to childhood.

Thinking about the times when things were good with her dad helped her ignore what was happening. She remembered the way he used to carry her on his shoulders and take her out back to swing on the wood plank that hung from the big oak tree. But that was before he got bad. She could remember the first day he came home angry, or at least didn't hide that he was. He slammed every door in the house and threw his cup at her mom, before ducking into his office and not coming out until much later.

She thought of her mother then. Helen was a saint—the purest ray of light in everyone's life, and so caring. She'd insisted that June should stay home after she turned eighteen—that she'd be safer waiting for a marriage proposal. Gods, if only she had listened to her mother. She didn't need to work, but she chose to, and look what that choice got her. Why was she so hell-bent on pushing boundaries?

June didn't notice that Don had finished and stood up until his deep chuckle snapped her from her dark fog. She let her knees slide out behind her and lay flat on the ground. Don crouched down and pulled a wallet from his pocket. Yanking five dollars from it, he dropped the cash in the puddle next to June's face.

"Keep the change, sweetheart, and let your father know I said hello."

The sentence didn't register for June, and neither did the cold that was still biting at her exposed lower half. Don pulled the silk from her mouth and began strolling down the alley. He whistled a jaunty tune that filled the air around them, and she began to sob again. Her wails bounced off the walls of the alley and rose up into the sky.

June lay flat on the ground, crying until there were no tears left in her. The wind drafting down the alley raised goosebumps on her spine and made her shiver. She pushed herself up to her knees, wincing at the pain of the rocks underneath her, and pulled her skirt down. Her mouth felt like cotton, and she licked her lips, finding them dry and cracked, before examining her hands. Seeing the pockmarks covering them brought on a fresh wave of tears.

She leaned against the wall of the alley, ignoring the wet slime soaking into the back of her dress, and placed her face in her muddy hands.

A rustle sounded nearby that she ignored. A moment later, soft hands reached out and gripped her shaking shoulders. She flinched hard and looked up to see a woman holding her hands out. June leaned forward and was pulled into her chest. The woman looked homeless, worn down by time spent in the elements. June felt too numb to care who was touching her now, and she let herself be held. Curling her hands into her chest and pulling her knees up, she felt so small. The woman stroked her hair and hummed, and June slowly relaxed in her embrace. She hiccupped one last sob out and the woman shushed gently.

"There, there, dear. I know." Her voice was like melted honey mixed in warm tea.

Although she wore rags, they were soft and warm against June's bare skin. She looked up and met the woman's eyes. They were a light hazel color, full of wisdom and pain. June sniffled and tried to speak, but her words were stuck in her lungs, her throat raw from crying.

"It's okay, I understand," the woman crooned. "The evil is gone. I have you now."

June curled up again and nodded. They sat together like that until the sun fully set and the marks faded from June's skin.

The woman stopped humming and whispered, "I know what it's like. I want to give you a gift." The sky suddenly crackled with lightning and thunder boomed, making June jump. The woman glanced up before dropping her voice further. "I bless you now."

Goosebumps raised on June's arms again. A cloud of warmth wrapped around the two women on the ground.

"Any man that dares gaze into your eyes with the potential to do you harm shall turn to stone before you." The woman leaned down and kissed June's forehead. "Just remember that revenge isn't everything, dear."

Thunder boomed nearby and June opened her eyes. She looked up to ask what the woman meant, but she was gone in an instant. Alone again, June looked around the alley as if seeing it for the first time.

She had no idea what the woman meant, or how she expected her words to help, but anger suddenly licked up the inside of June's stomach. How dare Don take her like that. How dare anyone hurt anyone like that! She stood quickly, filled with resolve, until she looked around again. Despair took over. Not a single person had come during the attack. No one heard or came to check on her. They had left her alone to be molested like some stray animal. She furiously blinked back tears and walked down the alley, back to the diner.

The closed sign was hanging in the door, but all the lights were still on. She pushed it open, the bell that announced her arrival barely piercing the veil of fog around her mind. Her feelings were a mess, beginning to muddle under a layer of numbness. That feeling held as Mr. Denny rounded the corner of the kitchen. His face was bright red as he stopped in front of June, placing his fists on his hips.

She flicked her eyes to the ground as he began to yell. He screamed, asking how she could leave work so suddenly, furious that she didn't warn him or leave a note. He had customers that had walked out from lack of service. He told her that she was an insolent, entitled brat and that she would never work there again. June continued to stare at the ground, his words barely registering. A buzz began in her ear and she raised her face in time to see Denny raise his hand, ready to strike her.

"Stop!" she yelled, the word slicing up her throat like a razor.

Denny froze in place, seeming shocked at the sound. His torso moved slightly, like he was trying to step forward. He glanced down, and a panicked expression replaced his angry one. June followed his gaze and sucked in a sharp breath.

His foot appeared to be solid stone. He tried to move again but the gray rock was quickly moving upward. His slacks looked as if someone had dipped them in concrete. He looked at June, fear clear in his eyes, and reached out a hand to her, his other one now stone by his side. In an instant, all his features were marble, and Mr. Denny was no more.

June was rooted in spot as she watched it happen, unsure of *what* exactly was happening. Her body went still as her boss was turned into a statue before her. She hesitated before stepping forward.

"Mr. Denny?" she whispered.

The stone didn't move. She reached up and touched his fingertip, which was hard and cold as ice.

June screamed, the sound echoing through the empty room, and turned, bounding out of the doorway and down the street.

June ran as fast as her legs could carry her, mind racing as the street around her blurred. She didn't know what had happened, but she knew it was something she did. Streetlights and houses flashed past her as her feet pounded the pavement. She turned left, then right, then zigzagged around a couple walking their dog, ignoring their puzzled expressions and the yelp that the terrier let out. She ran until a stitch formed in her side, slowing only when she ran straight into a woman smaller than her. She kept her gaze averted, careful to catch the woman's shoulder so she didn't fall.

"Are you okay?" The woman's question punctured through June's eardrums and caused a dull thud to start at the base of her skull. She nodded warily before picking up a jog, limbs aching and muscles screaming in protest. She moved as fast as possible until she reached her parents' house.

She hadn't visited in the two months since she moved out, but it appeared unchanged. The white fence outside still guarded the small front yard. The mailbox still proudly held her sloppily painted flowers on it. She carefully opened the gate, a giggle of disbelief erupting from her throat. Five steps took her up the walkway to the porch. Two steps up took her to the door, which she burst through. Nearly toppling over, she looked up and met her mother's eyes.

3

Helen stopped in the hallway, a basket of washing perched on her hip, when June pounded through the door. One look at her face and Helen knew something terrible had happened. She dropped the basket and reached out, confused. "Juniper?"

The girl ran to her mother, nearly knocking her off her feet, and fell into her arms.

"A man . . . he—" She stopped.

Helen shushed and rocked her daughter, eyes closed as she sent up a silent prayer to Apollo. With much difficulty, Helen moved her to the couch, where they curled up together. She pulled a blanket around them and rubbed her daughter's back, waiting until Juniper had calmed before whispering, "What happened?"

Juniper sniffled and looked up, pain obvious on her face. "A man, Don Whittaker, came to the diner. He—" She croaked and didn't finish her sentence.

Helen held her tight again, understanding. "Oh, honey, I'm so sorry. I should have been there." Her mind flashed back to all the times William had forced himself on her, and her jaw clenched. This was even worse.

Juniper shook her head but seemed unable to speak, her back tensed as if she was going to leap away and run. It was a long minute before she sniffed and whispered, "He told me to say hi to Dad."

Helen stiffened as her mind raced. Surely not. Was that a message? A threat? Who would hurt her little girl as a message? It couldn't be a debtor . . . William had a gambling problem, but it would never affect the family, right? She realized that she had stopped rubbing circles on June's back, so she resumed the motion again, trying to remember if William had ever said anything about a man named Don.

Now that she thought about it, William had never spoken about his activities outside of the home. The only way she knew anything was from going through the notes of debt in his desk drawer. Her heart thumped faster as her thoughts sped through the potential harm that could come, even aside from the attack on Juniper. What if they lost the house? What if they came for her next? For the first time in years, the numbness that shrouded her lifted. Anger rose and her cheeks flushed.

The man had changed that week June was born. He turned from a sweet and caring husband into every other abusive prick her friends spoke of. He drank until he turned vicious, gambled all their money away, and left marks on her body to the point she was forced to wear long-sleeve dresses daily. Everyone knew, even the neighbors. She had become numb to their gazes full of pity over the years, barely noticing when someone would stop in and quickly avert their gaze from a bruise peeking out of her sleeve. She had dealt with it all for the sake of raising their daughter together. She had settled for never upgrading their home, continuing to use their same old outdated dishes, worn blankets, and clothing, and never daring to ask for so much as a new hair comb.

He had completely checked out as a parent by the time Juniper was five. Thank the gods for Ty and his presence every few days, checking in and taking baby Juniper on walks to give Helen a breath. William had hated it. He had always held a strange grudge against Ty, as if they had had some terrible rift before Ty bumped into them in the neighborhood. She wished Ty had been around for her daughter tonight. She had excused all of William's bad features, choosing to shoulder the burden and shield Juniper from him, but now . . . he would risk their safety for his own selfish reasons. What was wrong with him! How could William do this? Allowing harm to come to their daughter was as bad as hurting her himself. When William got home, they were going to have a long discussion.

The moment came sooner than expected. Just as Helen opened her mouth to reassure June that she was safe now, she heard the front door open. Her entire body went still, and she flicked her eyes to the clock above the entryway. Dinner should have been ready a long time ago. This was the first evening in ten years that the smell of roast meat and fresh chocolate cake wasn't wafting through the house upon William's arrival. He seemed to notice too, as he stopped in the middle of removing his shoes and looked at the scene in front of him, apparently confused.

Helen didn't move from her position as her eyes trained on her husband. Her feet were pulled up on the couch, with June lying in her lap. They locked eyes and Helen flinched as anger took over his features. He lifted his shoe in the air and shook it at his wife. "What do you think you're doing?"

She began to answer, but he threw the shoe as hard as he could at her. She ducked her head and it hit the wall behind the couch with a dull thud. William balled his fists and moved toward Helen quickly. She managed to yell, "Will, stop!" before his hand closed around her arm. He dragged her upward, pulling her face an inch away from his, and repeated through gritted teeth, "What do you think you're doing?"

June slumped on the couch and Helen did her best to shield her daughter from William's view.

Helen, fully pulled out of her ten-year reverie, spat back, "Helping our daughter, William."

William threw Helen backward, causing her to fall to the ground. She caught herself and stood quickly, ready to challenge her husband. The smell of bourbon wafted from him, and she shook her head. "You're drunk. Go to bed."

William stepped forward and slapped her across the face. "You do not speak to me that way, woman." He stepped past her and eyed June still lying on the couch.

He scoffed and stalked into the kitchen, Helen trailing behind him. She planted her feet in the doorway as he looked at the empty stove. "Who the hell is Don Whittaker, and what was he doing at the diner?"

William whirled around, his expression unreadable. "How do you know that name?"

Helen jerked her thumb behind her and dropped her voice. "Juniper just came home from an interesting experience with him."

His face fell as he looked past his wife's shoulder.

"Maybe you should ask her what happened." She threw her words at him before turning to go back to June.

William's hand closed around her arm like a vice just a step out of the kitchen, and he yanked her to the hallway and threw her to the ground. Before she could react, he kicked her hard in the stomach, spit foaming at his lips as he screeched, "How dare you welcome me home—" he kicked again "—with an accusation and no dinner." He kicked Helen a third time and the veil that had previously lifted dropped back over her, forcing her senses to numb themselves to the pain of his foot connecting with her ribs.

She barely registered the bursts of pain as William leaned down and picked her up by the hair, dragging her back to the living room. She snapped back to reality as June stood from the couch and yelled, "Stop!" as loudly as she could.

William froze in place, eyes locked with his daughter. She had never said a word during these sessions with Helen before. Helen raised her hand and tried to croak out, "No!" but he stopped only long enough to let go of Helen and swing his arm around, hand balled in a fist, toward June.

His fist never made contact. Helen watched in amazement and mute horror as gray veins replaced blue, blonde hair turned white, and the sneer on William's face stayed there, frozen in time. William looked like a work of art—a terrifying piece, but art nonetheless. She reached out a hand and trailed it along the hard stone sleeve that hovered above her head, and her jaw dropped before a shudder forced its way down her spine. She quickly scrambled up and ran to June, hugging the girl tightly as they both stared at the statue that was William Georgian.

The women stood together like that for a long while. Helen said nothing about the prayers she had sent to the gods to get her out of her marriage for years, but her mind still raced. How did this happen? Was it divine intervention? Did June do something? No, that wouldn't be possible. It wasn't until the clock on the wall chimed loudly, alerting them that it was eleven pm, that she finally moved. She pulled away from June and looked at her daughter. June gave her hand a squeeze and Helen offered her a small smile.

"Dinner?" she asked.

June nodded.

4

A large gust of wind blew a pile of orange and brown leaves into the dark alleyway behind Mr. Denny's diner. As the wind settled, Typhon appeared, concern etched into his strong features. He could sense that other gods had been here tonight, along with June, and it made him uncomfortable.

Since he'd blessed June with protection, he could feel a pull of sorts on their bond, letting him know where she was and if she was okay, but he still couldn't tell exactly what was happening to her when he was away. The combination of more than one god's presence in the alleyway, along with her despair, had him seriously wound up.

He looked around for June, who was nowhere to be found. He took a step forward to walk down the alley when a shadow emerged from his left. Whirling quickly, he saw a drab, dirty-looking woman step toward him. Ratty clothes hung from her hunched body, and her eyes, which were the only bright thing about her, twinkled at him in the low light. Typhon inclined his head and smiled.

"Hello, Athena."

The woman chuckled and straightened, letting the disguise of dirty cloth fall off and reveal a toned, strong body clad in a leather skirt and chest plate. "Typhon. Tsk tsk."

Typhon's face fell as he looked down, examining the mud around them as she crossed her arms. "What happened?"

"Where were you?"

Typhon looked around helplessly. "There was a storm to attend to. I didn't know a couple hours would . . ." He trailed off and looked at Athena, and her face softened. She reached out a hand and patted his shoulder. He could only feel that June was hurt while he was gone, but not the extent of it.

"I couldn't make it before he hurt her. But I gave her something to help."

Panic took over the god's features as he tried to think of what on Olympus Athena could have done.

She laughed at his expression. "It's okay, Ty. She'll be fine. But next time . . . well, don't let next time happen. I may not be the one to come and take care of her." She gave him a knowing look and turned.

"Wait, what happened?"

She turned and looked at him again. This time, her features told a story of pain and exasperation. He got it now. She took one step forward, into a shaft of moonlight, and was gone, leaving Typhon alone with his thoughts. He needed to find June.

5

June carefully spooned bites of leftover stew into her mouth. The tender meat and spiced broth fell to sawdust on her tongue, and she had to force herself through the motions of eating. As she ate, she studied her mother's face, amazed. She somehow seemed younger, her shoulders more relaxed, and her eyes clearer than June ever remembered. For as long as she knew, she had wanted to get her mother out of this situation. She had begged Helen to move with her when she got her apartment, but the older woman was stubborn, insisting that running was never the solution.

Although the pain from the attack had cut her deeply, and she didn't know that she would ever fully recover, she was glad that her father wouldn't hurt Helen anymore. They ate in silence, each taking turns to cast a glance at William. Helen had drawn the curtains shut, making sure no one could see the statue in the middle of the living room.

Helen broke the silence first, bringing June's attention forward. "Do you think it can be undone?" Her voice sounded anxious, and June wasn't sure if it was because Helen wanted William back, or because she didn't.

She shrugged. "I'm not sure. I wouldn't think so."

Helen nodded solemnly and returned her attention to her bowl. Suddenly, she dropped her spoon, a look of horror on her face. "What do we do with him?"

June forced a small smile and reached across the table to squeeze her mother's hand. "I'll figure it out, don't worry."

Helen frowned, but she resumed eating.

The two women finished their dinner and cleaned up together in silence. Once finished, they stood in front of William and looked at him, sizing up how to move him. His face was eerie—frozen in the expression of rage he had when he had turned on June. One hand still hung down, while the other was in a fist, swinging forward. Dark veins ran through the marble, and where the light shone on it, the marble was stark white. June finally shuddered and suggested wrapping him in blankets before anything. Helen agreed and ran to the hall closet.

The two worked together to wrap him up, and when an old comforter was secured around his shoulders, June laughed. "Remember the time Dad got that awful flu and he went stiff as a statue from the fever? We were shimmying blankets around him then too."

Helen smiled, her eyes fogging a bit. "Yeah, I do." She seemed to drift to the past for a moment and stopped moving. After a few long seconds, she shook her head and continued wrapping blankets. A heartbeat of silence passed before Helen cleared her throat. "You know, he wasn't always a bad man. Once upon a time, he was truly amazing. He helped so much to prepare for your birth. I'm not sure what happened to him today—if you did something or a god decided to intervene—but I'm going to refrain from asking questions. I don't want to be involved unless you're in trouble and need help." She paused, and then looked at June sadly. "I just want you to know that he wasn't always bad."

June nodded slightly. "Thanks, Mom."

"I know it was hard to grow up with him," Helen whispered, securing a pillowcase over

William's head, "and I'm sorry I never had the strength to leave."

June reached out and caught her mother's hand, eyes hard as she looked her in the eye. "Don't ever apologize. You did your best, I know that. And quite frankly, I'm glad he's gone." Suddenly, a giddy giggle burst from June's chest, driven out by exhaustion and disbelief. "I'm GLAD he's gone!" she exclaimed.

Helen's face contorted strangely before she began to laugh as well. They both hunched over, an arm on each other's shoulder, laughing as the heavy air that had filled the house for years lifted. June felt lighter, and she knew Helen must too.

Helen recovered first, taking a shaky breath and pulling June in for a hug. "Thank you," she whispered into June's half-loose pile of curls. "I don't know how you managed to free us from him, but thank you."

June said nothing. She breathed in the scent of her mother—warm vanilla and fresh bread, now mixed with salt from tears—and nestled in, enjoying the embrace. She didn't know what she had done either, but she'd do it again if only to hear her mother's laugh—that laugh that had been reserved to a tight-lipped smile since June had learned to walk. She finally pulled back and motioned at William. "We should probably move him."

Helen's brow furrowed and she opened her mouth to speak, but June cut her off. "It's okay, Mom. I can handle it."

Helen's mouth set in a frown and she reached out to grasp both of June's shoulders. "Juniper Georgian, I have no doubt in my mind that you can handle anything thrown at you. You're the first woman I know to openly hold a job and live alone, for gods' sake! But, I'm worried. You shouldn't have to deal with what may come from this."

June smiled and mimicked Helen, placing her hands on her mother's shoulders. She thought they must look quite silly like this.

"Mother, it's okay."

Helen held her gaze for a long moment before sighing. "Okay. But you better take his truck."

"I've always wanted to drive something brand new." June grinned and wriggled her eyebrows.

Helen laughed, some of the tension in her shoulders dissipating. "I can comfortably say that neither your father nor I imagined his truck would be used for this when we went to pick it up last month."

June let out a low whistle as they walked through the side door and stood in front of the brand-new '26 Model TT. She rubbed the back of her neck as she looked over the shiny green paint and fresh tires. Since William had worked at a manufacturing plant, he had gotten a good deal. June wondered if it was actually related to the gambling, but she refrained from asking and risking the upset it might bring Helen.

June was exhausted, and with good reason. William weighed at least two hundred pounds, and it was well past midnight after dragging him through the house. But they still had to load William into the truck bed, so the two women moved to either side of his stone form. Helen reached up and pulled his head down, leaning his feet at an angle so June could get her hands under to lift.

Helen grunted. "Ready?"

June heaved her half of the stone up and the air in her lungs whooshed out as she shuffled to the truck bed, trying to keep her back straight. She was glad he wasn't as heavy as proper marble, but, gods, it was hard to carry an entire human-sized statue. She tried to set the foot end of him down gently, but a muffled clunk echoed out. She moved quickly to Helen's side and helped shove William into the bed.

When they pushed him in as far as possible, his head still hung over the edge of the tailgate. They stopped and looked at him. Good gods, if someone had told her she'd be moving her father's corpse in the middle of the night one day, she would have slapped them. This was unbelievable. Helen wrapped an arm around June and pulled her from her thoughts.

"Will you be okay? Would you like me to come with?"

She shook her head. "No, I'll be fine. Don't worry. But—" She pulled back and looked Helen in the eye. "It may be best not to tell anyone what happened. I don't know what exactly happened, but I don't want to risk the wrong person finding out."

Helen nodded and gave June one last squeeze before letting go. "Be safe," she whispered. June smiled and jumped into the truck, setting it in gear and rolling backward from the driveway. She gave a small wave to Helen before sputtering down the road. She would come back to check on her in a couple of days.

The drive only took a few minutes in the nearly new truck. It still amazed June just how fast they could travel with this year's vehicles. The last car they had was from before she was born. William had bought it in 1905 at release, and it was as slow as a snail compared to this.

June pulled up in front of the diner, parking parallel to the front door so it would be easier to pull William in. Once the truck was stopped, she gripped the wheel tightly with both hands, leaning her forehead against it. What was she to do? The woman in the alley had clearly been serious about her blessing. She thought back to how it had felt, like some divine power was around her, and wondered if the woman in rags had actually been a goddess. She sighed and lifted her head from the wheel, turning to look in the restaurant. What would she do with this place? She couldn't just leave it now that she'd basically murdered her boss, and Denny didn't have any relatives to speak of that would come around to take over. She didn't know how to run a restaurant, even if she'd practically been the face of it for two months. Plus there was Chef to worry about!

June finally let go of the steering wheel and turned to clamber down from the truck. As she reached for the handle and lifted her eyes, they met a pair of stormy ones. She let out a shriek and threw her hand to her heart before laughing. She popped the handle of the door and jumped out, nearly toppling Typhon.

"You scared the living daylights out of me!"

He gave her a sheepish grin. "Sorry, kiddo." He looked around and his brow furrowed. "What's going on here?"

June ran her hand up her neck, cocking her head and grimacing. "Um, I'm not really sure how to explain that." She pushed past Typhon and stopped by the bed of the truck. "This is going to sound insane, and you'll probably think I'm crazy. Honestly, I'm amazed Mom didn't—"

Typhon silenced her with a hand on her shoulder. "You would be amazed at what I find insane and what I don't."

June took a deep breath and nodded. She flourished her arm over William's statue. "Meet my new, and some may say improved, father." A nervous laugh forced its way through her chest, and she tried to cover it with a cough.

Typhon raised an eyebrow and pulled back the pillowcase covering William's head. As soon as he saw what lay under the cloth, his eyes widened and he swore, dropping the case and jumping back. "What on earth!" He whirled to June, and she shrugged.

"He needed a makeover."

Typhon groaned and scrubbed his face with his hands. "Are you seriously cracking jokes right now, kid? What the hell happened?"

June chewed her bottom lip and watched Typhon pace for a moment before moving to drag William from the truck bed.

"What are you doing!" Typhon exclaimed as she yanked William a foot toward her.

She heaved a breath and bit out, "Moving him."

Another hard yank on his neck and he was tottering precariously on the edge of the truck bed. His top half leaned down toward the ground and she leaped back, nearly knocking Typhon over.

"Shit!" she yelled. She bit the inside of her cheek as time slowed and William fell.

The solid stone statue crashed down against the slick pavement, knocking off his outstretched fist. June threw her hands up to cover her mouth as the fist bounced once before shattering into a thousand tiny shards, sending an echo slicing through the cool air. June stood rooted in place, staring in horror at her father's broken fist.

Typhon stepped up and cleared his throat, placing a hand on her lower back and causing her to jump. "Maybe I should help."

June shot a dirty look at his back as he stepped forward and bent down, gripping William by the middle and pulling him up.

"You couldn't offer to help before I broke my dad?"

Typhon grunted in response, pulling the marble out of the bed and setting it carefully on the road behind the truck. He turned around, and June noticed beads of sweat on his brow.

"I really hope there are no other surprises. We need to get him inside, then we'll talk about this—and your snarky attitude."

June wrung her fingers and grimaced again. "About that..."

She watched Typhon raise an eyebrow before she took his hand silently, leading him toward the diner. Luckily, Mr. Denny was positioned in just the right spot that he couldn't be seen from the street unless someone craned their neck through the window. June opened the door and stepped aside to let Typhon in. He stepped forward and gasped loudly. Taking a step up to Denny and looking at his face, he swore and whispered, "Athena..."

June snapped her head up. "What? What did you say?"

Typhon turned and looked at her, appearing to struggle for words. He released a loud breath. "Nothing. Let's get William moved."

June moved to block his path and planted her hands on her hips. "No, you said 'Athena.' Why?"

Typhon looked uncomfortable and he moved to step around her, but she mirrored his steps and raised her chin defiantly, looking her oldest friend directly in the eye.

"Ty, so help me. I have had a hell of a day, and if you don't tell me what you're talking about, I'll figure out how this thing works and you can join Denny and my dad."

Typhon's eyebrows shot up, and she bit her lip, wondering if she'd gone too far. He raised his hands in defense and muttered, "Okay, fine." He sighed and turned, pacing past Denny and back again.

6

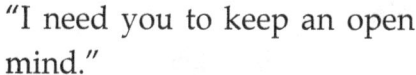

"I need you to keep an open mind."

June nodded, sliding into the booth across from Typhon.

"I am going to sound crazy."

"You didn't think I was crazy." June's eye's softened and Typhon's heart skipped a beat. He was about to share forbidden information with her, and she was totally calm. Well, he thought it was forbidden. He took a deep breath in.

"There is more to this world than what you see."

June rolled her eyes, but he ignored it, cleared his throat, and continued.

"You are an extremely smart girl, I wouldn't be surprised if you already knew, but my name is actually Typhon. I am the Titan God—"

"Of Wind and Storm," June finished for him. "We learned about you in school. I've wondered for years if you were really him."

Typhon smiled. Good old public education. "Well, there's more. I know about last night. But

". . . I didn't know about this." He motioned at Denny before reaching across the table to hold June's hand. "I'm so sorry I wasn't around to stop him."

June patted his hand in answer, face as stone-like as Denny's.

"I saw Athena after, but she didn't tell me what she had done. She was the woman in the alley."

At that, June's jaw dropped and she sprang up. "I knew it! I was thinking of her before, and I knew that woman was a god!"

Typhon grimaced. Were they all really that obvious? "Athena stepped in since I wasn't there, and while I don't agree with her methods, I am glad she could comfort you at the very least."

June opened her mouth, and then closed it. Typhon waited. Finally, she sighed. "I don't think you sound crazy. Somehow, I always knew."

"Normally, gods don't get in the way of mortal affairs, or even hang around a mortal life. But, I knew you would be special the day you were born. Your father did something so insane, so fantastical, that I knew his child would be both interesting and destined for great things."

June screwed up her face at that. "What do you mean?"

Typhon leaned forward, dropping his voice for emphasis. "He saw me . . . in my natural form."

June looked as though she ate something sour. "Do you mean naked?" she whispered, sounding horrified.

Typhon leaned back and let out a roar of laughter, his chest heaving and the sound bouncing off the walls around them as a small puff of wind swirled nearby. He laughed while June's face flushed. He choked on his laugh and coughed, shaking his head. He finally calmed enough to take a deep breath, the swirl of air next to them disappearing as he settled into a grin. "No, June. Even better. He saw me in my godly form. Not tethered to a human body."

June's jaw dropped yet again. "What do you mean? Like, just in the air?"

Typhon nodded. "Something like that. More like, made of air. The thing is, normally when mortals gaze upon a god that way, they go mad. They just . . . immediately lose their minds. The last one actually went on a killing spree."

June leaned back and Typhon watched a nerve twitch in her jaw. He furrowed his brow, worried. What if she didn't take this as well as it seemed a moment ago? Too late now.

"Do you think that's why Dad went so . . . bad?" She swallowed hard and looked at him, and his heart twinged again.

"I don't know." He watched as she picked at her thumbnail, her eyes glazing over. He had never really considered that, but it would make sense. He didn't want it to be the case. William had seemed so sturdy. He cleared his throat, and she snapped her attention back to him as he went on. "Either way, I'm afraid that you are now caught in the middle of something terrible. See, none of us had blessed a mortal in centuries. You were the first.

"When you were born, I blessed you with protection," he said in response to the confusion on her face. "Now, not only have I been involved, but so has Athena, and I wouldn't be surprised if some others step into play. They, uh—" He hesitated, embarrassed on behalf of his kind. "They're a nosy bunch and like to get involved."

June stared at him with a blank expression.

Typhon sighed. "Let me tell you a story."

June rolled her eyes and laughed. "Oh, a bedtime story? Love those."

Typhon reached across the table and swatted her shoulder. "Don't be a cheeky shit. Listen. A long time ago—"

June scoffed. "Does it have to be a long time ago? It's the middle of the night." She huffed.

Typhon crossed his arms and leaned back, raising an eyebrow until she waved her hand for him to continue. "A long, *long* time ago, the central three ruled Olympus side by side." Typhon paused and waited a heartbeat, but June said nothing.

"Zeus, Poseidon, and Hades. I'm sure you're quite familiar with Hades' story—sent to rule over the underworld, so on and so forth." June nodded. "Well, Poseidon was exiled as well. He tried to start an uprising against Zeus, wanting to rule more than just the seas. See, while Hades got souls and Zeus got mortals and Olympus, Poseidon was shuffled to the side, told to stick to water and fish, and, eventually, he grew bored.

"He sent some of his followers down into the underworld to steal from Hades. They took creatures of all sorts from him—terrifying beasts that had previously died and become experiments for new torturers. He stole from the other gods as well, taking prophecy from one of Apollo's oracles, wisdom and foresight from Athena, and recruiting some of Artemis' warriors."

June's eyes widened at this, but she kept quiet.

"Zeus found out, but only right before Poseidon raised an army against him. Much of Olympus fell, and good people died. We lost gods, Olympians, and titans, but inevitably, Poseidon lost. He was forced from the divine city and cast down to Earth. Some other gods followed, choosing to try the mortal, or semi-mortal, life, since it was something new and exciting, before returning to Olympus. Others went out of allegiance to him, but Poseidon was tied to a mortal body. Unlike the rest of us that may come and go as we please, he is stuck here, living many lives over and over again, his essence continuing from body to body until someone breaks the cycle.

"He's gotten worse over the years. Somehow, working out how to tie his lives together, he's grown powerful here on Earth. Now he heads the mob. He started the whole idea of it, actually."

June raised her hands, forcing him to pause. "You mean to tell me that a god is responsible for all the bad crap that happens here?"

Typhon shrugged. "Sort of. He's not tied to everything, per se, just . . . a lot. Since he maintains his soul, his essence, through all his lives, he holds the same memories, motivations, and ideals as before. But it's all gotten terribly worse. We've all watched him over time and believe he intends to fully conquer Earth as his own. To turn it into his own Olympus. While he really only holds this city right now, and some further south, he has set up such an intricate network throughout the country that he could very well take it as his. There's more to go into with this later on, but for now, there's this problem: all of us sort of have a marker that alerts other gods where we've been. Now, I'm not sure of *exactly* what happened in that alley, but I was shocked when I did some looking around, because along with mine and Athena's marks were Poseidon's." Ty paused and looked at June, who had a mixture of confusion and anger playing across her face.

"Don..."

Typhon nodded.

"You mean to tell me that *the* god, one of the top three, Poseidon, came here to . . . to—" Her words fell off and fury etched its way onto her face.

Typhon's throat bobbed. He didn't want to ask details, given her reaction, but he knew it couldn't have been anything good. "I'm not sure why. His involvement is so deeply entrenched here that it could be for any number . . ." He trailed off as June rose suddenly, turning to pace about the restaurant.

"A god would do that?" She threw her arms in the air as Typhon nodded.

"The big ones can get away with whatever they want."

June stopped moving and turned on Typhon, fire in her eyes. "No, they can't."

She dropped her arms and looked at the floor, muttering something that he didn't hear, before striding behind the service counter. Ty cocked his head to look and was shocked to see her emerge with a baseball bat. He almost laughed as he recognized the mark on it. He had gifted that to her to keep nearby when she worked at night, in case anyone tried to hurt her. Oh, the irony.

June strode to Denny and propped the bat on her shoulder. Her body shook and she loosed a loud scream that echoed off the diner walls, before dropping the bat down and swinging it wide.

It flew into Denny's ribcage with a loud shattering sound, and bits of his now stone shirt flew off, crumbling to the ground in a shower of dust.

"June—" Typhon half stood and raised a finger to try and bring her back.

He was cut off by another blow, this time to the side of Denny's face. His entire cheek and part of his eye socket fell this time, some of it getting stuck on his shoulder.

She dropped the bat and let the head rest on the floor as she screamed again. Typhon could hear the agony in her voice, and his heart thumped loudly. The power of her yell reverberated through the air and made his bones ache. He wanted to reach out, and stepped forward to do so, but she picked the bat up again, this time spinning to point it at Typhon. She let out a mirthless laugh, sounding deranged as she yelled, "If the gods want to play games, Typhon, then I'll play games!"

She spun quickly, taking the bat with her, and slammed it into Denny's leg, taking his calf out completely with one blow. Marble dust flew around her, coating her dark hair and already dirty dress, and making gray mud in the tear tracks down her face. The last of the bun that normally held her hair in fell loose, and her thick curls stuck out at odd angles, further contributing to the insane picture on display.

"June-bee?"

June didn't respond.

"Please, stop."

His plea fell to the floor between them as she moved to swing the bat again. He stepped forward once more and hesitated. Maybe space would be best. He had never seen her so angry. He could feel the air pushing against her in an effort to slow her down, and his tongue was heavy from the thought of trying to step in. He moved to the door as she raised the bat above her head and slammed it down on the tile floor, shrieking again.

The bell on the door sounded as Typhon brushed it with an air current, and she still didn't look. Typhon sighed and spun up into a puff of air, lapping around the diner once before whizzing under the door.

June screamed again, and Typhon carried the sound on his breeze as he floated down the street.

7

June finally regained her composure after nearly an hour. Her cries subsided to angry grunts as she threw her bat at Denny over and over again. When she was done, she stepped back, and the corners of her mouth lifted in a joyless smile.

In the time it took her to break nearly half of his body off, she had worked something out.

She knew who her dad had been gambling with now. It was the same person who had hurt her—Typhon had helped connect the dots. She didn't know what she would do with it yet, but it was something to hold on to. And she knew she had a strange, new power. It wasn't a fluke, it wasn't going anywhere, and she planned to use it fully. Funny, the girl who wanted to sculpt was given the power to make perfect pieces of art.

She looked over Denny, thoughts whirling, and touched the broken bits of him. He was now missing half his face, chunks of his middle, part of a leg, and both arms. The stone where she had smashed limbs off was rough and made him resemble the ancient works that sat in museums. He looked nothing like the Denny she knew. She supposed it was a good thing. If she was going to be using this power, it would be best if the statues were not recognizable. She didn't have the heart to smash her father to bits, though. And as unlikely as it was that someone would look for Denny, she knew her father had far more connections. She'd have to find a way to disguise him and craft a story. Maybe another visit with her mother would help. June breathed deeply, dropping her bat and looking around. Typhon was gone, and the diner looked like a demolition site. White and gray dust layered every surface. The service counter held bits of marble that had flown astray, and a deep pile of broken stone lay directly around her.

She shook her head, sending more dust flying, and grinned. Her arms were sore, this time from working hard instead of something she was forced into. She bent her knees and bounced a bit, giddy from the workout she had put herself through. She carefully stepped out of the pile of rubble and headed for the door. She stopped and turned to look over Denny one last time before flicking the light and exiting, making sure to turn the lock behind her and take the key.

She quickly walked to her apartment next door, enjoying the feel of the early morning air. Once in the middle of her kitchen, she breathed a sigh of relief. It felt like so long since she was here, even though it had just been the morning prior. Her breakfast nook still sat as crowded as always, the window overgrown with ivy vines and roses and the bookshelf behind the table stuffed to the brim with books, magazines, and notebooks. The table was a bit rickety but served her well. With only three chairs—because she didn't really need more than that—it fit in the nook perfectly, allowing a walkway into the sitting room. As she looked around the room, she felt like she had changed so much in twenty-four hours and was surprised to see that her home hadn't at all.

June turned to the kitchen and walked the length of it, stroking the countertop and looking around. She moved to the kettle and filled it quietly before setting it on the stove to boil. She sighed at the empty house as she busied herself making a steaming mug of coffee. She thought about how she'd have to clean up downstairs—and deal with her father. Shit, her father! She hoped no one noticed him through the windows.

Although, with the lights off, it should be fine until late morning. A diner really was no place for statues. And any sane person looking in would wonder what in the five realms had happened in there. She took a long drink and looked out the window. She really hoped Typhon came back. She knew it wasn't his fault that he left; she had gotten so angry.

She needed to visit her mother as well. Helen always had some sort of good advice, even if she couldn't follow it herself. She wondered if Helen might think that June was a bad person for turning Denny and William into statues. She wasn't even sure herself. She certainly hadn't intended to harm her boss, and her father, although always a mean person, probably didn't deserve such a fate.

As she raised her mug to her lips, a bit of stone dust falling from her head into the cup, a tap on the window caught her attention. She turned, but all she could see was the neighbor's ivy trellis. She raised her mug and the tap sounded again. Irritated, she snatched up the lock on the window and yanked it open. To her surprise, a large snake poked its head up. June stumbled back, nearly falling to the floor as she gripped the counter for support.

Snakes weren't common here, and certainly not ones like that. It had patterns in shades of tan and brown down its back, and its belly looked to be gold. When it dropped into the sink and the light hit its scales, it turned black as night. June opened her mouth, trying to find words, and she realized the snake wouldn't understand her anyway. It slithered across the counter to her mug, which it curled up next to. As it nestled its head atop its coils, it dawned on her that the snake was enjoying the heat from her mug.

June straightened, looking at the window and back at the snake. "What do you want?" she whispered.

The snake flicked its tongue in response, not moving.

She shook her head and walked back to the hall to go upstairs for a bath. She did not have the energy for this.

8

June slept fitfully for hours, from the time there were pink hues in the sky through its period of stark blueness, all the way until purple started tinging the edges of the horizon.

She woke slowly, bleary-eyed and more exhausted than when she went to sleep. When she got out of bed, her muscles groaned in protest. She took two steps before she had to lean down to examine herself. Heavy purple bruises were blooming on her knees, and bruises lined her hips and the back of her neck where Don had held her. She would cover as much as possible with a modest dress and hope that people wouldn't notice the others. Moving to the tall mirror in the corner, she looked at her face and frowned. Dark bags under her eyes screamed that she needed more rest. Her lips were cracked from chapping, and her eyes were as bloodshot as an alcoholic's. Her mind flashed back to the times she'd walked in to see her mother examining her bruises in a mirror, and she grimaced. Helen's skin was a bit darker than hers, and bruises only really showed for a day before blending in. For a moment, she wished she was the same.

Her mind drifted back to childhood, when she'd tripped over a large branch and fallen to the ground. Typhon and her mother had run over, crying concerns and examining her all over, and the attention made her burst into tears. She must have been around six years old at the time, and the following day, she proudly showed off her first large bruise to her father, reenacting the charge into battle she'd made with her imaginary friend. His mouth had set into a thin line as he nodded, but he didn't look pleased. June had heard him hit her mother that night, yelling about what people would think of him if she had marks like that.

She shook the memory from her mind and shrugged on her dressing gown. Going down to the kitchen, she was surprised to see that the snake was still curled on the counter. She rolled her eyes and moved to the living room to pull a dress from her clothesline.

By the time the clock struck seven pm, June was dressed and ready to deal with the task at hand. She vaguely wondered if Chef had tried to show up to work. June had the only key since Denny had put her in charge of opening and closing, so she imagined Chef would have simply left upon finding the door locked.

She moved quickly toward the diner, unlocking it and slipping inside before anyone could see. When she stepped in, she froze in her tracks, raising a hand to her mouth and letting out a small gasp. The place was a disaster.

She couldn't believe what she had done. She didn't have time to dwell on the residual feelings over her fit, though. June raced to the kitchen and pulled out a broom, sweeping the marble she tracked in with her as she went back to the diner's main area.

Cleanup was a grueling task, taking over an hour just to get the dust on the surfaces wiped up. Her scrubbing of the insistently sticky counter was interrupted by a knock on the front door. She stopped and set her supplies down gently.

"Who's there?" she called out.

A grunt of "Chef" came through the crack in the door, and June's insides twisted. What was she to do with him! Her mind raced. Could she let him in? No, he might recognize Denny. She couldn't keep him working and never seeing his boss. Would he believe her if she fired him? He had been talking about retiring, so maybe he would go early.

June cracked the door open, straining to block the view of the statues.

"Hi, Chef, how are you doing?"

He grunted and raised an eyebrow at her, peering past her small body. "Haven't seen Denny. Tried to stop in this morning."

June offered a small smile and met his far-off gaze. "Unfortunately Denny hasn't been around . . . I believe we may be out of work. I'm just cleaning up."

Chef grunted again and waited a moment before nodding. "Want help?"

June shook her head. "It's okay, I got it. Do you need the work? Last pay? I'll be grabbing mine from the till."

Chef's eyebrow seemed to raise even more before he glanced past her again and shook his head.

"S'okay, too much work anyway." He turned and took a step down the walkway, pausing only to call "G'night" to June before he disappeared into the night.

She breathed a sigh of relief and shut the door, making sure to twist the bolt into place. Gods blessed her tonight. Or Chef was scared by whatever he'd glimpsed. Either way, the knot in her stomach untwisted as she went back to work.

9

A light tapping on the door pulled Helen's attention from the book in her lap. Her eyes focused slowly as she realized that she had been reading for hours, and the sun had long since set. She set her cup of now-cold coffee on the side table and rose, stretching her limbs and wiggling her legs to bring some feeling back to her toes. She sighed and looked around. It had only been a day, but it sure was peaceful without William around.

She moved to the front door, taking her time. There wasn't anyone to yell at her to hurry and not leave guests waiting anymore, and she smiled at that. She swung the door open wide and a grin broke across her face as June fell into her arms.

"Juniper!"

"Hi, Mom," June whispered, squeezing tightly before stepping back. "How are you?"

Helen dipped her head and offered a small smile. "I'm okay, dear. And you? Would you like some coffee?"

June shook her head and followed Helen into the kitchen. The older woman busied herself with the kettle at the stove while she asked, "What's going on, dear?"

June leaned on the counter, summoning Helen's gaze. "We need to talk about Dad."

Helen fumbled the cup in her hand and it fell to the floor, shattering. June jumped back and yelped at the loud sound, and Helen's hands shook as she reached for the broom.

"Sorry about that. You know, it's been a strange couple of days."

June nodded, hand on her chest. "I know. I spoke to Ty, and I think we need to figure some stuff out."

Helen stayed quiet, working to steady her breathing as she swept up the fragments of broken porcelain. Finally, she stood. "I really don't know much. I haven't gone into your dad's office yet, and when I looked through a few months ago, there was a hefty stack of debt notes."

"I know, Mom, but we need to figure out what to do if anyone comes to collect. They already have once."

Helen clenched her fist around the broom handle and her stomach dropped. Her poor baby. She did not want to be reminded, but the comment struck ice into her chest. "I don't think we need to worry too much. William added my name to the house deed years ago. And I'm sure I could say he just ran off. We don't know where he is. Running away with a mistress is common nowadays, you know."

June shook her head. "I don't know, Mom, they came for me first. What if you're next? What if Dad has dug himself so far that he's past repayment?"

Helen's hand shook as she emptied the dustpan into the trashcan. She had already thought about that. She had thought herself in circles until she took William's emergency revolver and hid it in the pocket of her dress. She wouldn't go down without a fight. She turned back to face June.

"What do you suggest we do? Go to the police? Are we even sure what happened? Not to mention, the police are tied up in gambling rings here anyway."

June shrugged. "Let's start with the office."

Helen nodded, gesturing for June to lead the way.

The door to William's study swung open easily, revealing his span of shelves lining the back wall and a desk in the middle of the room. Helen took to one side and June the other, and they opened the top drawers in tandem, pulling out sheets of papers and rifling through in silence. After a few long minutes, June cleared her throat.

"Look at this."

She passed the paper to Helen, whose face drained of color. Along the top in red letters were the words: *Overdue Collection*. The statement that followed was unbelievable. Fifty dollars on one line. Thirty on another. One hundred and twenty! No, this couldn't be. She scanned the page front and back before her eyes snagged on the heading. "Whittaker Associations and Loans," she read out loud.

June cocked her head, and her expression was unreadable. "That makes sense. How much is the total?"

Helen swallowed hard. "Over a thousand. Overdue as of last month."

June leaned back on her heels and exhaled.

Helen turned back to her drawer and continued searching. Nearly an hour ensued that way, the pile of disposed papers between them growing and the pile of debt notes becoming uncomfortably high on the desk.

"Five hundred here."

"Two fifty."

"Another thirty."

A light tapping on the door startled Helen, and she stood quickly, almost prepared to see William standing there with a belt. She breathed a sigh of relief as her eyes focused on Ty's familiar form.

"Oh, Ty, I'm so glad you're here." She hurried over and gave him a quick squeeze around the middle. When she pulled back, she caught the tail end of an icy look shot his way by June, and she pursed her lips. Ty had always been like an uncle to her daughter, and she'd never seen them argue, but that was not a normal reaction.

"What are you ladies up to?" he asked politely.

Helen looked at June, who nodded. "Well, William isn't around . . . so we are trying to figure out a debt situation."

Ty nodded and raised an eyebrow, looking at June, and Helen's gaze passed between them as the air thickened. Finally, she blurted out, "What is going on?"

June sighed and stood. "Nothing, but he knows already, it's okay."

Helen took a deep breath and her stomach twisted. "Thank the gods." She turned to Ty. "I don't know what exactly it was, but he's gone. We are trying to figure out how to keep anyone from finding out . . . and why Don went for June."

It took effort to keep giddiness from her voice. Gods, she was a terrible wife for being grateful he was gone, wasn't she?

Ty nodded. "We'll work it out. What are we looking at so far?"

Helen swallowed hard. "At least three thousand dollars, just from two drawers."

Ty let out a low whistle. "Ouch."

10

The next morning, bleary-eyed and still sore, June dragged herself to Mr. Denny's desk. As much as her body protested after the grueling night of searching her father's office top to bottom, she knew that she should try and find some hint as to what might happen to the diner now that Mr. Denny was gone. It was hard to focus on the task at hand though, as a letter stashed in her pocket niggled at the back of her mind.

She hadn't mentioned it to her mother, instead choosing to slip it into her dress while Typhon reassured Helen that surely some of the debt would have already been paid off. The handwritten note on Don's letterhead contained an array of threats and intimate details of how Don planned to kill William. Frankly, she'd likely saved her father from an even worse demise. Her mind wandered to the letter as she worked in Denny's office, and she had to mentally shake herself to stay on track through the day.

Before she knew it, the clock chimed, announcing that it was nine pm, and June looked up from the stack of papers in front of her, shocked. Several hours had passed since she had begun sifting through the contents of Denny's office. As far as she could tell, his records were a disaster and the books had not been tracked in years. But two things were clear. First, Mr. Denny owned this building and her apartment outright. Second, he had no next of kin. This left June in an interesting situation.

Now, she was left with a pile of debt, a load of death threats, an empty restaurant that came with the deed to two buildings, and a choice.

She could go to the authorities and turn the deeds over for auction, or . . . no, she wouldn't consider the second option. Not yet, anyway. She wiped the back of her hand across her forehead, wiping a few beads of sweat off. Tossing the crumpled papers in her hand onto the desk, she decided it was time for a walk. She wasn't completely sure how deed transfers worked. She knew there wasn't much to it, really, just a single paper signing, but she wondered if Denny needed to be present . . . or if she could do it herself. There were plenty of forms in the desk that had his signature that she could copy.

She shut the heavy metal drawers that still needed to be searched and headed for the street outside, averting her eyes from the statues in the middle of the diner. Figuring out what to do with them was for another time, but they made her quite uncomfortable. As she turned the lock on the diner door, the cold night air brushed against her neck and sent a shiver down her spine, and she quickly flipped her collar up to protect against it. She should have grabbed a scarf, but she couldn't be bothered running to her apartment and up two flights of stairs.

A brisk walk up the avenue was what she needed. As her blood pumped and her cheeks flushed, she felt warmer and lighter. It wasn't healthy being cooped up around dead people. She still couldn't believe what she had done. She wasn't a violent person, and the fact that she'd flown into such a rage made her skin crawl.

She directed her thoughts away from her murder as she walked toward Central Park. Thinking about her dad and how different he was draped a sense of nostalgia around her, and she wondered about her mother. How would Helen keep the bills paid now that William wasn't around? June shook her head. Her mother was resilient and would figure it out. But June? She would have to shoulder what was left by William. It was her fault he wasn't around to deal with it after all. Screw standard roles, she was strong enough for both her and her mother.

A suddenly strong gust of wind blew up the back of her coat, and she wondered about Typhon. They hadn't really spoken since he took off during her rage, barely exchanging glances through the search of Henry's office. She wondered if he was mad at her. Should she be mad at him? Really, this whole thing could go back to being his fault ... right?

As she turned the southwest corner of the park, June heard a scream in the distance. She slowed her walk and turned to the trees beside her, listening.

"No, stop!" The words rang through the air clearly this time, and June realized it was a woman. Memories of her own cries while trapped under Don flashed through her mind, and she took off at a run, picking up speed as she wove through trees, crashing over bushes and breaking branches on her way toward the source of the call.

"Help!"

June broke into a sprint, a stitch forming in her side and heart pounding in her chest. She didn't know why she was running toward the scream instead of away, but her heart panged with concern for the woman. She slowed as she neared a walking path in the center of the park, and then she stopped, squatting and resting her arms on her knees. Damn, why didn't she ever take her mother up on the offer to join her women's exercise class? She tried to quiet her breathing, taking big gulps of air before holding completely still and silent for a few seconds. She listened for the call, but when a minute passed with nothing, June began to feel frantic. What if she was too late?

Finally, she heard the woman again. A garbled moan echoed from just a few meters down the path. June strode toward the sound, trying her best to move quickly and quietly so she didn't alert the woman's attacker.

Through a break in the trees, June stopped. The scene she faced nearly made her throw up as the memory of Don's cologne wafted around her. Lying on the ground was a woman, on her back, with her skirt pushed up. Although her stockings were torn and one of her dress sleeves was missing, she was clothed where it mattered. A large man, even taller than Mr. Denny, kneeled above her, knees braced between her legs. With a hand planted on either side of her head, June couldn't make out her face, but after a step forward she realized with horror that the man's face was forcefully pressed to the woman's.

She stepped closer and cleared her throat. The man raised his head and grinned lazily when he saw her. "Oh look, another friend." As he hoisted himself onto his knees, June looked straight at the woman, whose eyes were wide. "Did she invite you to play with us?"

His voice was unsettling, reminding June of the sound a teacher's ruler made sliding across a chalk tray. June forced a smile and nodded tentatively, and the man's grin widened. He stood swiftly and walked toward her, prowling like a cat that's cornered its prey.

"Oh how fun," he whispered.

He got close enough to touch June before stopping and straightening up. Every instinct in her body screamed at her to run, but she held her ground as he hooked a finger under her chin and raised her face to look into her eyes. Power, don't fail me now.

"Stop," she demanded.

The man didn't flinch, his finger continuing to trail down her neck. June looked at his feet and her pulse quickened at the lack of stone. Oh gods, what had she walked into? She whispered the word, and nothing changed. Maybe the power had been a fluke. She was about to go through another attack because she'd been too brave. Too stupid. The man's meaty finger scraped under her chin and she felt nauseous. She raised her face and met his eyes, holding her breath, scared.

He froze like that—hand held level with his chest and a finger crooked, posture relaxed, face smiling. She watched in mute horror as the last bit of his face faded to a dull gray. Somehow, the marble took out the terrifying air around him. When the last tuft of silky hair on his head was white, June breathed out and stepped backward. There had been no panic from him, no fear. Just the calm of a madman. She almost forgot about the woman as she studied his eyes, until she heard a gasp from behind the man. June leaned around and looked at the woman before rushing to her.

"It's okay!" She fell to her knees next to the girl, muddying her dress as she slid on the grass. "I won't hurt you. Just him."

Something strange flickered behind the woman's eyes, but the hard look glinting there was gone as quick as it came, and she let out a gasping sob. "How?"

June held out her arms and the woman's eyes widened before she fell into them. Her shoulders shook as if she were sobbing, but June couldn't tell if she was actually crying as a sprinkle of rain started above them.

"I'm not totally sure, but it worked. My name is June, and I came to help."

The woman nodded on her shoulder. It was a long while before she raised her head enough to say, "I'm Sarah."

Sarah pulled back and the women's eyes met. Something like electricity sparked between them, but June couldn't be sure. It felt similar to Athena. She offered a smile that Sarah returned and was about to ask what she was doing out here when a faint whisper rose from the grass nearby. She strained her neck with bated breath trying to see what the sound was from, and it wasn't until the creature was nearly upon her that she exhaled. The snake from her apartment was slithering toward her slowly. It reached her leg and promptly wrapped around it, working its way up to rest on the bit of her skirt that sat next to her. She flicked her foot to try and get it off, which warranted a quiet hiss, before it curled up. June swore under her breath, and the reptile seemed to wink at her in response. Hopefully, Sarah wasn't afraid of snakes.

June reached out and touched Sarah's shoulder, drawing her attention away from the statue.

"Would you like to come to mine and have a cup of tea?"

Sarah hesitated for a moment before nodding her head. "That would be wonderful, thank you."

June flicked her ankle and looked down, but the snake was gone. Maybe she'd imagined it. They rose together, clasped hands, and began picking their way out of the park. As they reached the main road, the woman suddenly looked at the sky and stopped in her tracks.

"I–I'm sorry, I have to go." She let go of June's hand and began backing away, yelling, "I have work tomorrow!"

As she turned and fell into a run, June stood in place, puzzled at the strange change, before shrugging and continuing on her way home alone.

11

As June walked away from the park, an idea grew in her mind. When she was a couple blocks away, the idea began to grow, and she turned back toward the park and the newly made statue.

What if she used the diner as an art studio? It was owned outright, after all. She'd have to ask her mother about the situation of a deed transfer, but really, unless someone came and questioned her for some reason, she could take the statues that she couldn't help but create and use them as reference for her own sculpting! It was brilliant, she thought. Her pace quickened as the rain drizzled down, soaking her dress.

That left her to figure out how to get Sarah's attacker back there. She was especially looking forward to shattering him to bits. She couldn't take the truck into the park, and frankly it was difficult to lift anything into the bed alone anyway.

She stood in front of the man, analyzing him. It was eerie, really, how serene he looked in death. So unlike her father and Denny, who had become panic-stricken in their demise. She wasn't sure if her power was speeding up its process, or if this one had been especially stupid and hadn't noticed the cold stone creeping up his legs.

She shook her head and grabbed the arm that was hanging by the man's side. Leaning him over, she began to drag the statue with a loud grunt. He weighed more than her father, and her muscles screamed in protest, having already been stretched to their limits by her bat exercise. She continued to drag the man inch by inch, legs wobbling underneath her, thanking the stars that the statues didn't weigh the same as proper marble. Gods knew how she'd move actual stone statues if she did take to sculpting on this big of a scale.

She stopped a few yards from where the man had been turned and leaned down, grasping her knees and wheezing. She was really regretting not joining those exercise classes now.

A great gust of wind blew in front of her, throwing bits of ivy around the man and swirling leaves at her feet. She straightened quickly, wincing at the onslaught of cold raindrops the wind threw in her face. She raised an arm to try and block most of it and rolled her eyes upon seeing Typhon appear in front of her.

He looked warily at the statue and back at her. "What do you think you're doing?"

June threw her hands up. "What does it look like? What are you doing?"

His brow furrowed in response, and he stepped up to grab the man by the arm and drag him. June wiped her brow with the back of her hand and smiled. Typhon grunted as he made the first pull, but he managed to move him a few inches more in one pull than June could. He stopped and blew out heavily, running a hand up the back of his hair and ruffling his shirt collar. A small current of wind spun itself behind him and underneath the statue's feet, lifting him up a fraction of an inch. Typhon grinned and winked at June as he began to pull the man along with ease, and she rolled her eyes at him again.

"Cheater," she muttered as they began to exit the park once again. She didn't know how she'd never noticed his wind tricks as a child.

Once they stepped out into the open of one hundred and tenth street, she became nervous, glancing around and back to Typhon.

"Hey, Ty? Do you think maybe we should pull him properly?"

The god shrugged in response. "I'm not too worried. People can't see past the glamor unless I let them."

Puzzled, she asked, "Glamor? What's that?"

Typhon laughed. "I forgot I hadn't told you! Most people can't see me. Or, they see something else. If I keep my glamor up, they won't want to come near me, and I'll just look like any other mortal. Unless another god, or someone close to a god, looks at me, we'll be fine."

June nodded thoughtfully. That was a handy tool to have. As they walked in silence, she thought back to the way the man's eyes had looked when she turned him. He'd been so calm, like he had expected her to come, or like he wasn't committing some terrible crime.

It dawned on her then. He started turning into stone once she'd looked him in the eye. That's what Athena had said too!

Her thought process was cut off as a car passed them. She stopped in her tracks as it parked on the other side of the street.

"Ty, doesn't that look just like Dad's old car?"

Typhon paused, looked over his shoulder, and shrugged. "I wouldn't worry. A lot of people keep cars for more than twenty years."

Still, she was unsettled. How strange that someone would have a car from 1905 in such a nice part of town, and especially one that looked exactly like her childhood car. She sped up her walk, and once they were another block down the road, she heard the car's engine sputter to life. A minute later, it rumbled by them and parked two blocks in front of them. The queasiness in June's stomach became worse as the car's engine shut off.

"I think we're being followed," she whispered, clutching Typhon's free arm.

He shook his head. "Don't worry, they likely can't see us. If anything happens, we can take off."

She nodded and resumed her normal pace. Typhon matched her stride, and the statue followed behind them.

The fifteen-minute walk home continued in the same way—the strange car would wait until it was a block behind, then park two blocks ahead again. Typhon seemed generally unbothered by it, but as hard as June tried, she couldn't shake her discomfort, especially with how dark the night was around them.

They finally arrived at the diner, and Typhon helped herd the floating man into place a few feet away from the others. June laughed, noticing the ivy wrapped around him like a boa for the first time. "That suits him."

Typhon agreed.

Once his current of air had disappeared, Typhon stopped and looked around. As he took in the look of the diner, he whistled.

June had cleaned up well and knew it. There wasn't a speck of dust left. She watched his eyes trace the tables and booths that she'd pushed against each wall. There was plenty of open floor now, and space to set stuff between comfortable seats.

"What are you going to do?" he asked, flopping into a bench.

June shrugged as she touched a loose bit of ivy on the newest piece of art. "I was thinking about converting this place to an art studio."

Typhon nodded and looked around. "I could see that. What about the boss's kids?"

June confirmed there were none, and Typhon looked around again, this time his brow furrowing as if he was thinking hard.

"You need some more art first."

"I'm thinking I'll use these statues for reference and carve them out."

Typhon shook his head. "That'll be far too much work. It could take months to get large enough marble here." He sighed. "I don't agree with the methods, but as long as you're only turning genuinely bad guys, I can get behind this."

June cocked her head. "This?"

Typhon motioned at the man from the park, and what he meant clicked in her mind. June gasped. "Really?"

Typhon nodded and she threw herself at him, wrapping him in a strangling hug. He pulled back after a second and studied her face.

"You look tired. Go rest. We can deal with this later." June nodded and turned to head up to her apartment. With Typhon on her side, this would be so much easier. An interesting venture, sure, but better than doing it alone.

12

June woke with a start, sweat beading on her forehead and sheets drenched in it. Her fingers trembled as she shoved away a stray curl that was plastered to her forehead. She'd had a nightmare about that night in the alley, and as the smell of cologne lingered under her nose for a moment, she rolled over to the edge of the bed as a wave of nausea overtook her shakes. She vomited all over her rug and wiped the remnants on her mouth away with a shaking palm. When was the last time she ate? She couldn't remember having any food after her meal with her mother, which was three days prior, if she was remembering correctly. She clambered out of bed and slid her feet into a pair of slippers, which, thankfully, had avoided her morning projectile.

After wrapping the rug up into a bundle, careful not to spill anything on the hardwood floor, she staggered downstairs and dumped the rug in the trash. She never liked it much anyway.

She washed her hands, fighting back more nausea, and then worked quickly to get the kettle put on. Tea first. That would settle her stomach. Then she would worry about food. Her intestines tied themselves in a knot as she opened her pouch of tea and the smell of ginger hit her in the face like a brick. Thinking about drinking her mother's sick remedy made her want to throw up all over again. She quickly turned the stove off and leaned on the counter, a trickle of sweat working down her spine. She wasn't sure what was wrong with her.

Opting for a piece of dry bread instead, she wolfed it down and immediately began to feel better. Then, as if on cue, the clock struck nine and a light tap on her kitchen window drilled through her brain. She turned to see the pest of a snake peeking through the glass and rolled her eyes. She couldn't deal with this today. Gods knew how she ended up with the wind as a best friend and a snake trying to adopt her.

She dressed quickly, doing her best to avoid her mirror. She did not need to be reminded of the sallow sunken skin around her eyes or the barely visible bruises still speckling her body.

She snatched up a pair of sunglasses and a notebook from the shelf by her table before heading outside. The last thing she wanted to do was accidentally turn someone in public, and in broad daylight no less.

Once out in the fresh air, she felt better. The sun was warm, peeking out of the clouds for the first time in days, and the breeze wasn't quite as chilly as it had been in recent weeks.

Today, it was time for a change in routine. She slowly wandered down the sidewalk, nodding as people passed by her. It amazed her that her world could be so shaken up while the couple that she passed could look so happy. She sidestepped around a streetlight and glanced across the street, brow furrowing as her eyes caught a man in a dark pinstripe suit across the road. She swallowed hard and kept going, choosing to ignore the tug in her gut.

She took her notebook to a café around the corner and settled down with a mug of green tea to brainstorm what she would do with the diner — and the statues it now held. Hunched over her sheet of scribbles, the warm atmosphere of the coffee shop began to soothe her. Her shoulders relaxed and the knot in her stomach eased as she scribbled her notes.

> *Art gallery? Can you sell . . . corpses male statues?*
> *Sculpt copies. Originals?*
> *Accents to art. Ivy/flowers.*

By the time lunch rolled around, she had an entire page of ideas written. As supportive as Typhon was, she was still uncomfortable over the idea of selling dead men. She'd like to explore the idea of sculpting if at all possible.

Suddenly, the hair on the back of her neck stood on end and a motion outside caught her attention. She glanced through the window on her right and her heart skipped a beat. The same car that had followed her and Typhon the day before was parked outside, across the street. She sucked in a sharp breath as her mind raced. Why were they here again? What should she do?

She carefully closed her notebook and stuck it in the pocket of her coat. Rising slowly against the wall to avoid the window, she tried to catch a glimpse of the driver before walking to the counter. She smiled sweetly at the woman working before leaning in to whisper, "Hi, I was wondering if you had a back exit?"

The woman gave her an odd look before pointing to the right side of the café. June nodded and said thank you before weaving between tables and walking through the side door.

Her breath caught in her throat as she stepped into an alley.

Flashbacks slammed their way into her mind and she crumpled on the ground, choking back tears. She couldn't stop the images from moving in front of her eyes, and the unmistakable smell of his cologne wrapped around her like a blanket, suffocating and slowly choking off her airway.

Tears streamed down her face and the door snapped shut behind her, forcing the walls of the alley inward. She tried to protest the overwhelming feeling of despair to assure herself that she was okay, but she felt as if she was drowning. Lights flashed in her vision and a roar filled her ears. The ground rushed up to her and water from a dank puddle soaked into the seat of her skirt. A voice echoed from somewhere nearby, but it was muffled by her sharp inhale at the cold assault on her skin.

In a flurry of movement, someone in a dark coat ran up to her, crouching and placing their hands on her shoulders. June flinched and screamed, her eyes unable to focus on the person in front of her. All she could make out was a light, golden face and dark shapes under that.

"Hey! Are you okay?" The voice finally broke through the barrier around her, and her eyes focused.

In front of her was a man—around her age, it seemed—with warm, brown eyes and mousy hair that was just a little too long. He wore a dark gray suit with a navy coat and black scarf. June sucked in a breath as she realized he wasn't hurting her and tried to stifle her tears. "I-I just—" she stuttered, and the stranger squeezed her shoulders and moved to help her stand.

"It's okay. What happened?"

June wiped the salty tracks from her face and steadied her breathing. "Nothing, I'm okay."

Looking side to side, she finally saw that the alley was not closed in, or dark. Two large, clear exits sat on either end, within ten steps. She laughed and hiccupped, her breath ragged from the sudden crying fit.

"I'm okay," she repeated, this time to reassure herself.

The man in front of her gave her a look of concern before nodding firmly and releasing her shoulders. "Do you need any help?"

June pulled in a stuttered breath and shook her head. She looked around again, double-checking the ends of the alley. "N–no. Thank you."

He gave her a small smile before trotting back down the alley. June watched him go, confused, before turning and walking in the opposite direction. She had to get away before the car figured out where she was.

The walk home only took a few minutes and, luckily, there was no sign of her assumed stalker. She looked curiously around as she stopped outside her front door to pull a few letters from her mailbox before trotting inside. As she rounded the corner to her kitchen, she stopped dead in her tracks. There, on the counter, was the snake.

"What are you doing here?" she demanded.

The reptile seemed to smile in response, and she paled. She had to be going insane. Talking to a snake like it would respond, randomly throwing up—that's it, she was losing it.

She snatched a bowl of leftover pasta from the fridge and threw a glare at the snake before going to curl up on the couch. She had so many things to deal with, but after the flashbacks and strange man earlier, she couldn't be bothered.

As she tore open the first letter in the stack, her stomach dropped. It was a bill addressed to Mr. Denny's Diner. Electricity was due, and it was more than she expected. She set the letter on her side table and opened the second, which made her nauseous all over again. Another bill. As she rifled through the stack of mail, they were all bills that she had to pay.

She set her face in her hands and breathed out shakily.

She needed to figure out a job, and quickly. There was no way she could afford to live without an income. Her mind wandered to her mother. Helen had taken up sewing . . . maybe she could too? And when she was really young, her mother had sold paintings. She thought about the statues downstairs and wondered if anyone would actually buy them. She couldn't sell dead men . . . right?

She forced herself to take a few bites of cold food as she pondered all the possibilities of her future business ideas when it suddenly hit her. She practically owned this building now. She didn't have to work much at all! She'd found enough money in the safe during her search of the office to live for at least a year, if she was frugal. She'd pretty much run the place for the last few months as Denny had ducked out. She doubted anyone would bat an eye if the business was turned into something else.

She became giddy as she started to imagine opening an art gallery. Charging a few cents for admission would be enough to get her by, but she needed more statues, and in different poses. Not everyone would enjoy the looks of fear on Denny and her father's faces. And she certainly couldn't sell William anyway.

She set down her bowl on the side table and rushed downstairs, flipping her glasses off her head as she went. She needed the wind to find Typhon and tell him her plan.

As she swung the front door wide open, she nearly ran into a solid mass standing on the other side. Dazed, she looked up to see the stranger from the alley standing there.

"Hello." He half raised a hand in greeting and held a sheepish grin on his face. "Sorry to startle you. I just wanted to check in."

June blinked at him, confused. "How did you find me?"

The man shrugged. "I turned around at the sidewalk and saw you walk this way. I was worried after you . . . you know."

June nodded slowly, starting to feel uncomfortable. She leaned through the door, looking to the right and then left. About a block away, the car that followed her was parked. She quickly pulled herself back inside and muttered, "Sorry, have to go," before slamming the door in the man's face. She breathed heavily as she counted the seconds after closing it. Anxiety gripped her like a vice and her mind raced, wondering why there was now a man and a car following her. Maybe the car belonged to him? No, that wasn't likely. He seemed nice. He'd helped pull her out of panic, after all. And she had never met him before. He didn't have a reason to.

She waited a few long, painful minutes before cracking the door open again. He was gone, but the car still sat in place. They surely weren't connected.

She snatched a wide-brimmed cap from the hook by the door and yanked it onto her head. She made sure every stray curl was tucked up inside it before wrapping her scarf high around her nose and ducking outside. She sprinted down the road in the opposite direction of the car, and when she slowed to a walk, she turned to make sure she was alone. The car hadn't moved and was a speck of black many blocks away now. June fell into a comfortable pace, heading for Time's Square, and whispered "Typhon?" as a breeze blew over her face. She wasn't sure it would work, but she hoped that he would hear her.

As she rounded the corner of forty-fifth street, a swirl of warm air brought her friend down into a slow walk next to her. She pulled down her scarf to say hello, and he threw his arm around her shoulder in response.

"What do you need, kiddo?"

"I think we need to find some bad men."

He nodded, and she began to lay out her plan. She wanted to find a few more men to take to the diner, but she needed to catch them when they wouldn't realize what was happening. Then she'd give the diner a coat of paint and open it as a gallery. "I can sell them for a couple hundred dollars each, I think. Only the bad guys, of course," she said hastily, noticing the twisted-up look on Typhon's face. He relaxed and nodded.

"I can help with the first one." He took her hand and began to lead her down a side road toward a building being constructed. "See that place there?"

June looked where he pointed and noticed the unfinished building. Steel beams stood upright inside a rough brick wall that stood a few feet taller than Typhon. She nodded and he continued.

"The guy building that didn't pay his employees, instead running with the money to have this apartment building constructed."

June became angry as she remembered her own father having his pay cut and how it affected her family. Then she remembered the man in the park. She hadn't known anything about him. What if he'd had a family? What if this man did?

"Are you sure? I don't want to do this wrong."

He nodded firmly. "He's paid directly by our favorite so-called god. He's directly responsible for a minimum of nine homeless families. And he took advantage of his secretary."

June gritted her teeth at that and asked, "Where is he?"

Typhon pointed to a little house a few yards from the building. "He sits on the porch there to read the paper right about this time, every day. I've been watching him for a while, planning on a storm to take down what he's built."

June gave Typhon's hand a squeeze and whispered, "Thanks," before he started to spin back up into the breeze. She grabbed his arm quickly and he stopped, eyes wild and hair windswept. "Can you ask Mom about the deed?"

Typhon nodded and raised his hand to wave, but his fingers had already disappeared in the breeze. June gasped and released his arm, and he was gone in a poof. She quickly shook off her shock at watching him fade into wind and strode to the gate in front of the house.

A clean walkway bridged the gap over manicured grass and neatly lined flower beds to the front door, and sitting in a wooden chair to the side of that was an old man in a tan wool suit. He was bundled up with a brown scarf pulled up to cover his chin. She could see his bulbous red nose, likely inflamed from too much drink, and his bloodshot eyes over the top of the newspaper.

She swung open the gate silently and crept toward him, purpose set, and an image of crying workers painted in her mind. She stepped up on the porch in front of him and cleared her throat. He didn't move.

"A-hem!"

He finally raised his eyes to her, face still pointed at the paper.

He was stark white in an instant. Gray speckled his nose and eyes where red had been, and a look of boredom was etched on his face. His newspaper was the only thing that didn't change, the top corner of one of the pages ruffling in the wind.

A thrill went through June's stomach. She thought he looked like a proper work of art.

13

Typhon whirled down on a coast of leaves in front of Helen's familiar front yard. He slammed down harder than expected, feeling unbalanced after June's interference in his shift. He straightened, pulling his cap down over his short hair and rubbing the bit of it peeking out at his nape. He sighed as he looked at the house. Whenever he'd visited here throughout the years, it always held a dark air. Last time, though, he'd actually felt welcomed by the whitewashed exterior. It was as if William had bled his anger into the walls of the house over the years, and it only dissipated when he was gone.

It was welcoming again today as he strode up the steps. He didn't have much time, needing to help June move the statue before she was caught on that man's porch with a perfect copy of him. Typhon's lip curled as he remembered watching him turn away his now-homeless employees. He really deserved what came for him.

Typhon reached up and rapped on the door, and a moment later an out-of-breath Helen swung it open. He arched an eyebrow at her disheveled appearance, and she smiled sheepishly.

"Typhon, dear, what can I do for you?"

"I came to ask something about the house deed — on behalf of June."

"Oh." Helen breathed, her wide smile dropping. Her brow furrowed and she looked nervous.

Typhon glanced behind her but couldn't see anything in the dark of the hall. "Am I interrupting something?" he asked, and her shoulders sagged.

"I had a date."

Typhon pursed his lips and nodded, trying hard not to judge the quick rebound after William's demise a few days earlier. He knew they hadn't been intimate in years, thanks to one night that Helen had a bit too much cooking sherry and let loose a stream of secrets.

"It'll be quick. We just need to know, when Will signed your name to the deed, was there a witness present?"

Helen shook her head, concern etched in her face. "No, the magistrate said we could do it at home and it would be honored by the bank if anything ever came up."

Typhon nodded and smiled.

"Great, thank you." As he began to turn away, a familiar voice carried through the crack in the door before it snapped closed. A shiver ran down his spine as he assured himself it wasn't who he thought.

He shifted in the wind and was gone in a burst of orange leaves. His essence smirked as he looked down through the breeze and watched them fall. Not every god got to leave a physical mark with their hop through reality, but he loved that he was different. He chalked it up to old age.

14

Typhon appeared next to June as she finished separating the man from his seat, and she jumped as his feet hit the wooden porch.

"Good gods, Ty!" she exclaimed, and he smirked.

He blew out a light breath and it worked its way under the man, caressing his back and ruffling the corner of his newspaper. They stepped out onto the road together and June glanced at her friend, concern taking over as she noticed his jaw clenched.

"What's wrong?"

He sighed and the statue jumped a few inches in the air. "I ran to your mom's like you asked . . ."

June nodded, waiting. He paused and the wind settled again.

"She was with someone. It seemed as if I . . . interrupted them. The voice sounded familiar, but I'm not sure."

June's brow furrowed and she was lost for words. Her mother rarely ever had company, but she would be surprised if it was a man. Not that William gave her much of a relationship. She wouldn't be upset if her mother had found good company already, just surprised.

Typhon touched her arm and the corner of his mouth twitched up. "Want to try something fun? I need to work off some steam."

She raised an eyebrow but didn't protest as he wrapped his fingers around her arm. The air around her lurched and her stomach dropped as they seemed to jump into the air. She felt as if her limbs were expanded away from her and a current of electricity speared her chest in half. Nothing hurt, but it felt very strange. She closed her eyes against the force from above and opened them when it felt like they stopped moving.

June tried to gasp but nothing happened as she looked down at the ground that was now a hundred feet below her. She didn't so much hear Typhon's chuckle as felt it around her. She tried to speak but couldn't feel her mouth, and a moment later, she was zooming through the air.

She closed her eyes against the assault of wind passing through her, and seconds later, it settled. She looked down again to see the ground rising slowly—or perhaps she was descending. Time slowed as she fell to the dirty concrete, and she gasped when her feet collided with the ground.

She stumbled to the left and a strong hand caught her before she fell. She blinked rapidly and looked around. Typhon grinned at her before bursting into laughter, and she swatted his hand off her. Irritated, she stepped away.

"What was that?" she demanded.

Typhon's laugh faded and he motioned behind her. She turned and gasped again when she realized that they were standing in front of the diner.

"That was a shift, June-bee. It's how we travel."

June spun around and looked at him, brows furrowed. "We?"

He shrugged. "You know, gods."

June wrung her hands and nodded. It was easy to forget what he was sometimes.

Typhon motioned to the diner door, his current of wind pulling the man with the newspaper behind him and inside. June paused for a moment before following, trying to swallow and force her stomach back into place.

Typhon set the marble form down a few feet from the others, and June stood awkwardly in the doorway.

"How'd you enjoy the trip?" Typhon asked.

"Maybe give me a bit of a warning next time," she grumbled.

Their eyes met and Typhon grinned before they both burst into laughter.

June's eyes glimmered as she laughed, a tear forming in her eye. It felt good after the events of the week. She finally stifled it down, clutching the stitch in her ribs as she went for her baseball bat. She wanted to preserve as much of him as she could, but she felt like he simply needed to lose a bit of back weight.

"Do you need anything else, kiddo?" Typhon asked, voice still airy.

June shook her head. "No, I got it."

"I've got some work to do this week. I'll be back later with another location."

June didn't say anything as a light breeze tickled her cheek like a kiss. She turned around to see the door swing shut, before cleaving her weapon down hard and fast, carving out the back of the newspaper man's head. She clenched her jaw as she lifted the bat again, this time moving clear down his back. She continued over and over until she carved out a fairly even patch of rough rock and the back of his coat and trousers were gone.

As she examined him, she swore she could still see the tans of his outfit and red in his nose. She knew she was imagining it, but it was a strange phenomenon as she touched his smooth face. As she studied his features, she realized that as good as it felt to break these men down, someone might recognize them. She'd have to come up with an explanation for how they came to be.

She had to think long term now if she planned to sell these instead of sculpting her own. Looking around the diner, she thought about how many more pieces she would need. Maybe she would put her father outside as a welcome—a bit of a scary welcome, but nonetheless. She would leave the other three staggered on the right side of the diner, which left space for five more.

She cleaved the bat down again, this time aiming for the left side of the man's head and taking out most of his bulbous nose. She smirked at the man, reveling in the power she held over him.

She had some more collecting to do.

15

Typhon drifted on the wind above Miami. He watched as people walked around the city, to and from work, to the bank, to the park with their children. They all acted as if today was another normal day. Poor mortals.

He didn't particularly enjoy this part of his job. His mind wandered to June as he picked up the winds and began swirling them through the city, trying to shoo people back into their homes. He wondered what she was doing now. He had pointed her in the direction of a bartender before he left, hoping that he might be the last man she needed to complete her collection. He was truly worried about her.

Since they started seeking out victims together a couple weeks prior, something had changed. She was no longer the shy girl that aspired to be a famous sculptor. She had developed a taste for revenge after Poseidon hurt her, and it seemed that the more people she hurt, the more she enjoyed it.

He was sure that he was being dramatic, but it really did seem that she enjoyed the game.

He looked down on the beach as a woman in a light-blue dress tried hard to shut her front gate and protect her flower garden behind it, but the blowing gales kept swinging it open. His brow furrowed. Why did mortals always try to save the most ridiculous things during natural disasters?

He picked up speed as he moved with the wind, bringing water up from the ocean with him and waiting for the lightning to begin from Zeus. Normally, once the first strike knocked down a building, people began to realize what was going on.

He had already hit the islands south of here, and he thought that Miami would have been prepared. As he swept up stray umbrellas, hats, and rubbish in his wake, he wondered at the scene playing itself out in front of him. His winds buffeted the sides of houses, and different men and women were working quickly to pull in strangers from the street. A little old woman hobbling with a cane was quickly ushered into a restaurant by a young man in a black suit. Another woman grabbed an abandoned baby carriage and wheeled it into her house.

Typhon worked quickly, trying not to look too closely at the destruction he caused, as he tore through the greater Miami area. Water rose to knee height and the winds picked up even more.

He truly hated bringing storms like this, preferring to spend his time in parks, twirling leaves on a breeze for children to chase. But, sometimes, humans became too hungry and cities became too populated, and disaster was necessary to bring them down.

His mind wandered as he swept through the city, and he remembered a similar storm nearly three centuries earlier. Before Poseidon had become such a dick, he'd been quite helpful with this type of work. As much as Typhon understood hating your responsibilities, he thought that the jaded god of the sea would enjoy manipulating water to destroy mass amounts of architecture. But the last storm they whipped up together, Poseidon went rogue in protest. They were supposed to be sweeping out a mass of diseased desert, and he had instead turned on a brilliant city. The residents were ahead of their time. Absolute geniuses, the lot of them, and Poseidon buried the entirety of the city under a chunk of what is now Spain.

The last that Typhon had seen of that city — Atlantis, he thought it was called — was Demeter acting on a favor she owed Poseidon and growing a mass of trees over the area. Typhon shook his head in disgust. A massive loss, for no reason. He shouldn't dwell. That was Poseidon's way, after all.

Finally, before Typhon reached out to strike another wooden building, Zeus threw down a bolt on the one next door. Typhon grimaced at the message and threw his arms up, directing the storm higher, faster, and further across the city. His last thought before bringing one-hundred-and-fifty-mile-an-hour winds down on the soaking wet buildings was of June. He hoped she was okay.

Typhon's blow struck, and the city went dark.

16

June sat at the desk in her new office, scribbling notes about opening the shop. Her plan would move forward in just one day, with *The Evening World* newspaper printing an ad to direct the wealthiest people around New York City to her newly converted art gallery.

She had managed to gather all the pieces of art she needed in the weeks leading up to this. It had been difficult, but it was worth it. Since Typhon disappeared after their third find together, she had branched out on her own. Things had become desperate, though, as she was running out of places to find terrible men. Her most recent was a man at the park holding a squishy rubber ball that whistled at her. She had turned on him so quickly that the ball didn't have time to leave his raised arm. He had become her final piece a few days before. She may have overdone it on filling the gallery, but it would be okay.

It was strange, though. The more she used her power, the easier and more comfortable it was.

The men she froze changed more and more each time. Now, as she looked at them, they froze in a matter of seconds. The stone climbed their bodies so fast that the impact would cause fractures or pieces of marble to flake off. She no longer needed the bat, as she could easily break bits of their faces or hands with a light tug. Unfortunately, this also meant that they had to be carefully wrapped before she dragged them back to the gallery.

She stopped writing her last line as a familiar whispered slither echoed around the display room. She dropped her pen and the ink splattered, blotting out the $200 she had written next to the title *Man with Child's Toy*.

She walked out of the office and into the gallery to see a strange image. The snake, which had continued to pester her of late, was stretched between the statue of the man with a newspaper and the man crouching. The snake's pointed tail barely touched the edge of the latter statue, and the rest of its body was stretched taught on the floor, with its head wrapped around the former's foot.

June laughed and asked, "Are you measuring my placement?"

The reptile hissed in response and moved its body to sit between the bartender and Mr. Denny.

Setting her mouth in a frown, she moved to try and shoo the snake, but it raised its head and nodded while its tail flicked toward the bartender.

She blanched. "You want me to move him?"

The snake nodded and flicked its tail again, before laying it down and wrapping it around its body, leaving only four inches of snakeskin pointing out. June rolled her eyes and threw her shoulder against the bartender, inching him closer to Denny. Ridiculous, she thought, as she pushed. That thing was going to be the death of her.

She shoved and shimmied until the snake gave a satisfied flick of the tongue, and she stood, looking down and straightening her dress. When she looked back up, her friend was gone. She laughed and wondered if maybe she was imagining things, before returning to her desk.

17

Light dawned through the gray shield of clouds, a shaft of it reaching through a gap in Helen's bedroom window and falling directly across her eyes. She smiled sleepily as she squeezed her eyelids tight against the brightness. She was in no rush to leave her bed today.

In the weeks since William had gone, she felt so much lighter. The fog that had settled over her through years of enduring his abuse was completely gone, and she felt like a new woman. She took some time off work, thankful for the hidden sock full of cash under her side of the bed, and finally relaxed for the first time in years.

The company she'd been keeping had helped, of course. Gods, she couldn't believe her luck at bumping into her new favorite visitor at the grocery store. Her toes curled remembering their last night together, and the smile on her face turned wistful. She reached behind her and remembered her bed was empty, and her grin dropped.

She'd been left alone the day before, her new partner insisting they spend a few nights away. An ache settled in her chest as she thought of them.

She hadn't been one hundred percent sure that they'd make a good match at first. It was the first time she'd met someone that looked male but preferred not to be called that. She didn't totally mind. The way they made her feel when they were around was more than worth adjusting her language. Their first dinner together had proved that they had much in common, and she held no qualms with changing her way of thinking.

She rolled to face the space they had laid in before. Her fingers brushed the pillowcase that she'd replaced after William left. A bit of guilt trickled into her stomach, but she bit it back as a frown took over. Sure, she was still technically married, but did it have to be a bad thing that she found good company? She deserved that, right?

The door creaked behind her and she lifted her head enough to see her new partner stepping in. She smiled and propped up on an elbow. "What are you doing here?" she asked, the early hour making her voice raspy.

They smiled and leaned down to peck her cheek. "I missed you and thought I'd come to cuddle."

Helen smiled and turned back to their pillow, waiting for them to lie down. A heartbeat passed but they didn't move from behind her. She started to lift up again. "A—" Something dark swooped over her head and cut off her voice. The air turned cold and dread seeped into her bones. The last thing she remembered seeing as she lost consciousness were a few specks of gold left on the pillow from nights before.

18

The day of June's grand opening dawned with the sun in the sky and not a sign of autumn on the breeze. The gods must be looking out for her, as she threw open her bedroom window and enjoyed the warm rays of light on her face. Maybe Apollo was wishing her luck.

She took her time getting ready. Everything had to be perfect. She stood in front of her mirror, clad in a silken robe, and carefully applied her makeup. She didn't normally wear it, as the colors that were available didn't suit her tanned skin well, but today was special. She gently dabbed some cream into her eyebrows, smoothing them down and brushing the hairs in a downward slope, before pressing her eyebrow pencil to the tails to lengthen them. She spit into her cake of black cream and rubbed a brush in it, before swiping the flat bristles upward through her eyelashes. A quick line of dark pencil went onto her lash lines.

June carefully applied her red lipstick, making sure not to go outside the natural lines of her lips. While she loved the shape of her mouth, thin lips were all the rage right now. She smudged the same color into her cheeks to finish off and slowly packed away her products. She stepped back and examined herself. She supposed that she could be called pretty, but with the brightness now accentuating her features, she didn't quite feel it.

She dropped her robe and allowed herself a moment to examine her body. The bruises from Don had long since faded, and she was beginning to develop muscle lines from her constant moving of heavy statues. She frowned at her reflection. She had to stop building muscle. It wasn't normal for a woman to look like this, and the last thing she wanted was to stand out.

She dressed quickly, putting on her finest dress that fell to her shins and a pair of black heels. The faster she didn't have to look at her nude body the better.

Once downstairs, June moved to make a cup of tea, but a heavy wave of nausea washed over her as she set down her mug, and she had to grip the kitchen counter to keep from toppling over. She stumbled to the sink and her dinner from the previous night bubbled up, splashing around the ceramic basin. As she spat and began to rinse the sick down the drain, the clock chimed, letting her know that it was eight am. She washed her mouth quickly, hoping that her lipstick was still intact, and snatched up a piece of dry bread to settle her stomach as she ran down to the gallery. She didn't have time to ponder why she was sick for the first time in weeks. It was time.

June stood in the doorway, looking over her display with satisfaction. Each statue was spaced evenly apart. The old diner tables lined the walls, separated by booths, all of which had been recovered with a nice, neutral cloth. Plants decorated each surface, including the old checkout counter, leaving enough space for people to pay for their art. The kitchen had been converted to accommodate the barista that would arrive soon.

She stepped up to Mr. Denny and examined him. As her first piece, she had grown attached. She had spent extra time draping the perfect amount of ivy over his body, bringing some color to the stark white and dark gray of his new body. She reached up and straightened the sign around his neck that read, "Make an offer." A knock on the door tore her attention away.

June flipped her sunglasses down and swung the door open wide to a girl not much older than her. She smiled and stepped in.

"Did you order a coffee maker?" she said with a chuckle.

June relaxed her shoulders and smiled, before leading the girl through the now-doorless kitchen entry. She showed the girl, who introduced herself as Amy, to the coffee pots and pointed out various things around the kitchen that she may need. Amy assured her that she would be fine to figure it out, and she got to work setting out sugar and clean mugs.

June returned to the checkout counter to double-check that everything was in place. As time ticked down, she could hear the clamor of people outside the door. She rubbed her hands together nervously and forced a breath in and out to calm her nerves. What if nothing sold? She was down to fifty dollars in the register, which would only keep the barista employed and herself fed for a couple of weeks. She breathed in and out again. It would be okay.

Two minutes to nine now. June moved to the front door and plastered a large smile on her face. It was time.

She pushed her sunglasses up the bridge of her nose and swung the door open wide. To her surprise, at least thirty people stood outside. A collective cheer went up and June quickly composed herself, propped the door open, and began to greet the people as they walked in. All sorts had come to visit—men, women, men and women with children. Everyone was dressed nicely, and nearly everyone looked surprised to see June standing there. She assumed that they hadn't seen a woman opening a gallery before. Or perhaps it was her color. Either way, they were polite as they entered. Things had steadily been changing around here for years, and she hoped she didn't look out of place.

As she was about to go back inside to mingle with her guests, a sleek car stopped in front of the building. Confused, June paused and watched as a chauffeur stepped out of the driver's seat and opened the back door.

A gorgeous woman stepped out of the car. Clad in a long fur-lined coat, white stockings, and black heels, she looked like someone that should be on the silver screen. She wore heavy makeup and a head wrap that accented her chin-length coifed hair beautifully. As she approached June, she smiled brightly, before stepping past and strutting up to the statues. June felt as though the wind had been knocked out of her and took a moment to breathe deeply again.

As she went about the gallery, speaking with the visitors, she was pleased to hear compliments over and over again on her work.

Mr. Johnson simply couldn't believe the amazing detail in her carvings.

Mrs. Harding was confused that they were all men, but impressed nonetheless.

As the hours passed, people came and went, and June's hope began to fade. No one had put an offer in yet, all seeming to have come just to look. As noon neared, she noticed that the beautiful woman from the nice car was still sitting in a booth, sipping coffee. June approached her and smiled, clasping her hands behind her back.

"Is there anything I can help you with, Miss . . . ?"

She held out her hand, which June took and squeezed gently. "Hi, darling. My name is Louise Brooks."

She pointed to the statue of the bartender, who still had the vacant expression on his face from when June had asked if he could serve a wet martini. "Is that one there for sale? I'd love to have him stand in my dining room."

June's heart skipped a beat as she nodded. "Yes, ma'am. Just put an offer in, and I can get the paperwork drawn up."

Louise nodded and thanked her, before reaching for a slip of paper and pen from the table next to her. She quickly wrote a number down and folded it in half before handing it to June, who inclined her head, thanked her, and walked to the register. She unfolded the paper there and felt the air in her lungs whoosh out and tears begin to sting her eyes.

Written in beautiful script on the small scrap of paper were the words *Eight Hundred*. June set the paper down and braced her arms on the counter, breathing hard. Eight hundred dollars? That was more than her old wage for an entire year. Oh no, that was too much. She looked up and saw the woman watching her, and quickly ducked under the counter to grab a certificate to fill out. She took a few seconds crouched on the floor to even her breathing out.

Once filled out with the date, sale price, piece number, and a few other details, she took the paper to the woman, who motioned to the man with her. He yanked a stack of bills from his jacket pocket and handed them to June, who, with a look of amazement on her face, curtsied to Louise and breathed, "Thank you, Ms. Brooks."

Louise smiled at her again and rose to leave.

The afternoon moved quickly after Louise left. More men and women came through as another wave of them left. She swore she saw the familiar back of a navy coat bobbing about the gallery, but she couldn't be sure, and couldn't remember exactly where it was from.

One more offer came in, which distracted her from thinking of the odd coat. This offer was for five hundred and twenty dollars, and it was for the statue of the man who attacked Sarah. June accepted it graciously, filled out the paper, and carefully tucked the roll of bills into the back of the register.

She began another circuit around the room, her breath catching as she stopped behind a couple.

The woman leaned into her husband, clutched his arm tight, and whispered, "I swear that looks like Daniel. His face is a bit mushed, but look at the pin on his jacket! It looks just like the pin Macy gave him."

June's breath hitched and her heart rate picked up as she stepped closer. The man shrugged and grunted, and she clenched her fists in between the folds of her skirt. She stepped beside the woman and cleared her throat.

"Anything I can help you with?" she asked sweetly.

"Oh! No, I think we're okay. I was just saying that this one looks very much like my brother."

The air whooshed out of June's chest and the walls seemed to move in a few inches as she looked around. Her nails dug painfully into her palms and she plastered a smile on her face, hoping no one could see the bead of sweat skating down her spine.

"Well, I tend to sculpt based on people I've seen." Her jaw clenched as the woman's eyebrows knit together, and she sent up a silent prayer.

The woman turned back to the statue of the man bending to retie his shoe, his face turned up at the perfect angle, as if he was looking at her to speak.

The woman turned and smiled. "It's just . . . you have such an eye for detail."

June relaxed a fraction, unsure if it was a genuine compliment or if the woman was suspicious. "My Daniel even had a pin he wore all the time like that—a gift from his late wife." She motioned to the oval disk that sat a bit further out than the man's jacket.

June jerked her chin down. "Yes, ma'am, I try to capture everything that I can."

The woman's eyes misted over and June's stomach flipped, stress raging through every muscle.

"It's just a bit strange as I haven't seen him in over a week. I've tried to visit him a couple of times, but he's been away." She turned back to the statue again and traced her fingers over the broken side of his face. "Odd . . ." she murmured.

June looked around helplessly, wishing Typhon was here for a moment and scrambling to find something to say before the woman cleared her throat. June turned her eyes up and met a small smile.

"No matter," the woman murmured, before her voice picked up. "It's just a funny coincidence."

June nodded and smiled, shifting her weight to stand partially in front of Daniel. "I'm sure you'll see him soon. I may have just caught a glimpse of him before he left town or something."

The woman smiled wider and nodded, reaching out to squeeze June's arm before moving away.

June sighed heavily and turned to study Daniel herself. She'd have to be a lot more careful in the future. Identifying details like that could really hurt her business. Not that much could be done as far as an investigation goes.

June felt eyes on her back and she turned, sucking in a breath as her gaze landed on the man in a gray suit and blue coat. She cocked her head and he smiled at her crookedly, offering a small wave before he turned and walked through the door.

She moved to follow him but suddenly Amy appeared in front of her, grinning from ear to ear. "A celebratory cup of coffee for our artist!" She laughed and June couldn't help but join, her general unease fading.

"Thank you." She tapped the rim of her cup against Amy's. "And cheers to the best help I could have asked for today."

Amy smiled brightly again before scurrying back to the kitchen, and June resumed her walk around the room.

The afternoon wore on, and people continued to trickle through the door. June nodded to them, offering smiles and answering questions about how she'd come into this line of work. She tried to be as honest as possible, and she enjoyed the conversations, but as soon as the last person left, she fell into one of the booths and kicked off her shoes, a sigh of relief slipping through her lips.

A gust of wind blew open the door and June looked up to watch Typhon walk in. He scanned the room, noting the barista through the window, before turning and greeting June with an excited smile and clap of his hands. "Big success today, right?"

June smiled in return and nodded. "Yes sir! Two gone, and a world of possibility ahead!" She stood to hug her friend, then held her hand out to the remaining statues. "I'll have to fill in the gaps now, but imagine if this works! I'll just keep cycling my art through and be set forever!" She laughed, but Typhon pulled back, concern obvious in his features. June's smile faltered. "What?"

Typhon glanced at Amy again and his voice dropped. "Bad people only, though, right?"

June shrugged flippantly. "Yeah, of course." She moved to the register and Ty followed.

"June, you can't take anyone you want." His voice became even lower, with an edge to it that made June uncomfortable. "Who's the man with the ball? That's a child's toy he's holding!" he hissed.

June looked up at him defiantly. "It doesn't matter, Ty, don't worry about it." She began counting the cash in the till, leaving out enough to pay Amy. She heard Typhon scoff as she kept her eyes averted, and when she looked up, he was gone.

Her body sagged, and she worried for a moment that her best friend was leaving her, but then Amy peeked around the corner and asked for her help. Typhon would have to wait.

As she looked around the gallery once more, it occurred to her that Helen never came. June had dropped an invitation in the week before, and she was sad that her biggest support in life wasn't there to see what she'd accomplished. Perhaps new freedom had caused her to forget.

19

Long after everyone had left the gallery, including Amy, June stood in the middle of the room, broom in hand, staring blankly at the man with the newspaper. Typhon's concern was on her mind, and she tried to shove it away to see what all her patrons had. She couldn't find the beauty in the marble, although the hundred or so people that had visited did.

She reached a finger out and traced the darkest gray line trailing across the man's cheek when a sound from behind her made her freeze. She gripped the broom with both hands, prepared to swing it at whoever was there.

"Well, well, well, Juniper, what on earth has happened here?" A deep, silky voice echoed off the statues.

June spun quickly, jaw dropping, as she found herself face to face with the most interesting person she had ever seen. They were tall, towering over the statue of Mr. Denny that they stood next to.

Thick black hair slicked back with a rich smelling oil fell to their nape. The stranger's eyes, although warm, were snakelike — slanted and gold in color — and made their dark skin glow. The effect was further intensified by a smattering of gold glitter around their eyelids and cheekbones and shimmering lipstick that fell into a line down their chin.

They wore the strangest black suit. Stiff and shiny, it appeared to be made from the skin of an exotic reptile. Even their shoes were scaly. *Regal* was the only word that June could think of to depict the picture of elegance standing in front of her. The odd-looking person bowed their head in greeting.

June stuttered out, "Who are you?" and inched toward the front door, prepared to run.

The intruder laughed. The sound was warm and pleasant and reverberated around them. They threw their arms out in a dramatic flourish. "Don't you know, girl? I'm your guardian angel." They bowed deeply with a sweeping motion. "Pleased to make your acquaintance, ma'am. My name is Asclepius. Although — " they raised their head and their eyes twinkled under an arched eyebrow " — we have met before."

June stopped her shuffle away and cocked her head as she noticed the faint buzz around them. It felt as though the air was charged with static, and there was almost a halo of light around them.

"You have the same feel as Ath . . ." She trailed off, realizing that Asclepius wouldn't know what she meant.

But it seemed that they did. They nodded and a grim expression flickered over their face. "Dear old Athena. She was banished and had her powers taken for crimes against Olympus, you know." They gave June a pointed look, as if it were her fault. They waved their hand airily. "Nothing to concern yourself with. You're hardly expected to know the rules."

She chose to ignore that. "How am I expected to know you?"

Suddenly Asclepius spun, and their body seemed to fall in on itself. As they moved, the scales on their shoes climbed, melding together with the strange black suit. The scaly sheath writhed and twisted together, and a slithering sound filled the air. After a few seconds, a large and familiar-looking snake with black scales that flashed gold lay coiled at June's feet. She gasped loudly and threw her hands to her face while Asclepius sprang back up from the pile of scales and yanked the collar of their suit jacket back into place.

June sank to the floor, exhausted, trying to wrap her mind around what she just saw. The snake that had followed her for weeks, pestering her, sneaking into her house, and being an overall nuisance, was yet another god. She placed her head in her hands and fought back a wave of dizziness.

"What do you want?" she muttered.

Asclepius seemed not to hear her question as they stepped up to the man holding a toy and looked at him.

"Who do we have here?" They looked at June with a raised eyebrow.

She looked up, dropping her hands. "He whistled at me and almost hit me with that ball."

The god's eyebrow went up further, and they pointed to a statue with its arms outstretched and a surprised expression.

June jumped up and laughed in disbelief. "He threw a flowerpot from an upstairs window down the road. It almost killed me, so I turned him."

Asclepius stopped in place, hand still outstretched, fingertip on the man's wrist. "Why . . . why would you do that?"

June blanched in response. "I had to! He almost killed me!"

Asclepius burst out in laughter. They took a moment to calm down before fully turning to face June. "And you're sure of that?"

She nodded slowly, confused.

The god gave her another pointed look, and her confidence wavered. They circled the man once before speaking. "Us immortals can't stop the stream of time, you know. We simply ride it. Let the fates weave what they will. You should too, but here you are . . . interfering more in human lives than any god."

"But I have the power to stop bad people. I should use it."

They whirled on June. "No, girl, you shouldn't," they hissed, stepping closer to June.

She held her ground and lifted her chin defiantly. "Maybe I just have better morals than you."

The god narrowed their eyes. "Oh, honey. You think you're so special? You're not. You look at the clouds floating by and see them as wisps. Don't you realize that even though they have the power to give life through rain, they also hold the power to snatch it away just as easily? Should they do that every chance they get? What would happen to the world if a torrential downpour took hundreds of lives every day? Everyone has power to some degree. Even fragile girls caught in dark alleys. It's how you choose to use your gift and knowing when the right time is."

June tried to protest "But Athena—"

"Tsk. Athena didn't give you some wonderful power or terrible curse. She simply opened your mind to the possibilities that already lay within."

Asclepius walked away, rounding each of the marble statues scattered about and looking at them. "Don't you see, girl? You have become the very danger you feared, simply by using that power every chance you can. Look at all this destruction!" They spread their arms and June's eyes widened as she took in the men standing in different places with pieces of their bodies missing. It was as if she was looking at the room with completely new eyes.

The golden god paused for a moment as understanding dawned on June. Then they pointed at the man with the ball. "He was a father and was expecting a second child. He meant you no ill will, and he was whistling to his son to catch the ball." They motioned to Mr. Denny. "He found out his mother died the day you were attacked. Even being the fuddy-duddy that he was, he wouldn't have struck a soul any other time."

Asclepius approached the flowerpot man, studying his face closely. "This one accidentally nudged that flower off the sill. He was trying to catch it when you killed him."

They turned and faced June, hands on their hips. "Don't you see? Not everyone meant you harm. You simply took their words, or expressions, or body language, and magnified them to turn them into a villain in order to justify your own end game."

June stared at the god, shock overtaking her features. Her mind went blank as Asclepius chuckled. "You're playing with fire, girl, involving yourself in things you don't understand." Their eyes narrowed. "Maybe you should focus less on murdering men in cold blood and more on your mother."

On finishing their last, snarky comment, the god collapsed back into snake form and promptly disappeared into thin air.

20

In the weeks that had passed since the attack, June had mostly pushed the nonsense of gods out of her mind. The strange anxiety attacks were easing, as were the flashbacks. But her fits of nausea had re-emerged, which she couldn't quite figure out, and it worsened at the thought of any of the gods.

For the tenth day in a row, she sat in the café around the corner, drinking a cup of green tea. She had found lately that it was the only thing that helped with her sickness. Today, she had a notebook in front of her and was writing a list of potential places her mother could be.

The week before, with Asclepius' words floating around her mind, she had gone to visit Helen. Her mother hadn't been home, which wasn't unheard of. Plus, June had gone in the middle of the day. She remembered that Helen had mentioned traveling, so that was a possibility. She didn't want to worry herself for no reason, and writing ideas always calmed her, so she had come to the café every day since, from seven am until she had to open the gallery.

Rain pattered against the window at her back, casting a cold echo on her heavy peacoat. The shop smelled of fresh pastry and frothed milk, the latter of which worsened her sick feeling, but the atmosphere here was so warm that she ignored it, lulled into a sense of security at her normal table.

She wondered if maybe her mother was down in Miami. She had always wanted to go, after all. She sighed. How she wished Typhon were around. She hadn't seen him since their spat, and she could really use a friend.

She flipped her page over and began scribbling down painting ideas. She was down to five statues, and she would soon need to put out other purchasing options. Both Asclepius and Typhon's opinions on her collection had made her uncomfortable, enough so that she didn't want to turn anyone for a long time, unless she saw them really do something terrible. She didn't want to be the villain in anyone's story. Plus, with the recognition of Daniel, she felt as if she were on the brink of getting in terrible trouble.

Her train of thought faded as movement down the road caught her eye. She turned her head and her eyes trailed on a car that looked eerily similar to the one following her. She breathed a sigh of relief as it rolled past. Only the front was the same. She took one more long look out the window and turned back around.

When she spun her head, she let out a loud yelp, jumping a few inches in the air. Opposite her, where there was previously an empty seat, now sat a man in a mismatched gray suit and navy coat. His sandy hair flopped over his brown eyes, and he had a crooked grin plastered on his face as he leaned over the table, mere inches away from June.

Her hand flew up to her heart and she tried to steady her breathing as she glared at him through the dark lenses of her glasses.

"Can I help you?" she asked tersely.

He sat back in the seat. Removing his hands from the edges of the table, he dropped his smile a bit. He paused for a moment before he jutted his hand out, this time holding it at an angle to shake hers. She looked at him again, baffled by what this man was doing, and placed her hand gently in his and gave it a light squeeze. He looked vaguely familiar, and the color of his coat coaxed the memory buried at the back of her mind, but she couldn't quite place it.

"Can I help you?" she asked again, this time with an edge to her voice.

"I've been following you. I work . . . I mean, I—"

June watched in bewilderment as he blushed.

He whispered, "Let's try again," and snapped his mouth shut, stood, then walked out the door.

She shook her head in amusement at the strange behavior and looked down at her notebook for a split second before the bell clanged on the door, drawing her attention back up.

The mismatched man strode back in, scanned the café, spotted her, and waved. "Hey there!" he called. The patrons nearby looked up at him, confusion and discomfort clear on their face. June couldn't help but smile as he stopped behind the chair opposite her and placed his hands on it.

"Hi! My name is Henry." He stuck his hand out to shake hers yet again. She obliged. He pulled back and continued. "I'm an investigator with the police department. May I sit here?" He motioned to the chair, and June's heart rate sped up as she nodded cautiously.

Henry sat and leaned forward slightly.

June cleared her throat and asked, "What can I do for you, Henry?" This time, she tried to keep the ice from her tone. Her mind was racing and bile rose in her throat.

He offered her a smile and stage-whispered, "We're doing great," before straightening up and stating in a normal tone, "Well, Mrs. Georgian, my boss has some questions about Mr. Georgian and his whereabouts."

June's small smile faltered, but she quickly regained her composure. "And, what, Mr. . . ."

"Chekov."

"Mr. Chekov, what do those questions have to do with me?"

Henry leaned forward, an air of playfulness still around him. "Honestly, I'm not sure, Mrs. Georgian, but I'd like to find out. May I buy you a coffee?"

June shook her head. "No thank you. And it's just June. Mrs. Georgian is my mother." She did not need to owe a police officer for a cup of coffee.

Henry nodded his understanding and made his way to the front counter. The second he was gone, June let out the breath she had been holding. Who was this man? Why was he asking questions? She watched as he dug a handful of coins from his pocket and counted a few out onto the counter for the barista. As he gave the woman making coffee another of his goofy grins, a memory smacked her in the face.

Back in the alley of this same shop, this man had helped her. Plus, he'd shown up at the gallery for a brief moment. She knew him, although it had been a few weeks and she had been so busy that she forgot his face. She didn't remember him being quite so handsome, though. Then again, she hadn't looked at his face much. But now he was here to question her. There were only two potential outcomes here, she thought. Either she told him the truth and he was so interested in the situation that he'd drop the issue, whatever it was, or she lied and risked him investigating her further. How do you tell a stranger that you turned your father into a marble statue? Oh yeah, you don't, because that sounds insane.

He returned then, interrupting her thoughts by resuming his seat. "They'll bring mine over soon." June nodded and clasped her hands on the table, bracing herself to come up with answers for the man.

He mimicked the movement and began in a friendly tone. "Well, Miss Georgian, my boss would like to know where Mr. Georgian has been. He's tried to see him multiple times with no luck. The man apparently hasn't been at work either." Henry's eyes twinkled as he leaned in and gave June a mischievous grin. "And I would like to know, Miss Georgian, why you are wearing shades inside on such a miserable day. And what you're writing in that notebook." He nodded down at her notes, prompting her to scramble to cover them up, clasping her hands on top of it.

Her mind galloped faster than a racehorse and her heart felt as if it were going to merge with her stomach. "Well, Mr. Chekov —"

"Henry, please."

"Well, Henry, my father has become indisposed. He's simply not in a state to talk to anyone. I'm happy to answer any questions on his behalf. As for your second question, I'm afraid I must ask one of my own. Do you intend me any harm?"

Henry looked taken aback and shook his head furiously. "Gods, no! I assure you, I am just doing my job. I find you rather intriguing and would only hazard an interest in your . . . quirks. I would never hurt you."

Puzzled, June asked, "Quirks?"

Henry looked a bit sheepish as he explained. "Well, I've seen you in this café quite a bit. Part of my job the last month or so has been to follow you. I noticed that when you're not here, you're doing strange things, and strange things have been happening around you.

"I watched you cart the most interesting marble statue into a boarded-up diner and follow it with hundreds of plants. Meanwhile, it seems you haven't noticed a massive snake trailing you. I swear I watched him wink out of existence one day and appear ten meters from where he was previously. Frankly, June, I'm intrigued."

June blinked once at the grin on his face and tried to think of what to say. Icy fingers curled their way around her insides and her mind raced while moments of silence stretched between them. Who on earth would notice Asclepius? Wouldn't they cloak the same way Ty did? And how did he see the last piece move? That was in the middle of the night!

June finally cleared her throat and began to move, picking up her book and finishing her tea in one gulp. "Perhaps my mother would be better suited to answer your questions."

June got up and began to walk away.

"I'm not sure where to find her," he called after her as she reached the café door. "I tried their house, and it's been empty for a while. That's why I thought you might be her!" June froze and her heart stopped. She didn't know that the house had been empty. She'd known about the last week, but that was it. She swore she'd seen her mother two weeks earlier.

For a brief moment, she considered turning to ask Henry what he meant, but discomfort steered her through the door. The last thing she needed was this man asking questions or gaining any incriminating information from her. She shook her head and kept going, walking straight down the road toward her parents' house.

"Please be okay and be home," she whispered over and over into the breeze blowing past her. As the cold air nipped her nose and cooled the back of her neck, she pulled her collar up. For the middle of autumn, the weather had been strange. She continued muttering her prayer while she wove through the blocks of midtown. Left, then right, then straight for five minutes, until a heavy breeze pushed June forward a step faster than natural and brought Typhon down next to her. He stepped down to match her stride and they walked quickly down the leaf-strewn path together. June shivered, and Typhon waved his hand, quieting the cold air that was forcing goosebumps down June's spine. She turned and offered him a small smile.

Typhon inclined his head and tipped his beaten-up driver's cap. She giggled a bit and the tension between them dissipated.

"Tell me, Ty, why do you always wear that ridiculous thing?"

Typhon feigned offense and threw his hand up to his chest, blanching at her. June laughed and shook her head, keeping on with her steady pace. "I don't think it's ridiculous," he muttered. "It matches the suit."

June eyed him up and down, then shrugged. Sure it did. His three-piece suit was tawny in color, same as the cap but in much better condition. He wore dark-brown leather shoes and a dark-brown tie.

"I'm very stylish, I'll have you know." He said it so matter-of-factly that the corner of June's mouth raised.

It dropped again into a frown as they rounded the corner near her mother's house.

Typhon looked confused for a moment before stopping and asking, "Why are we here?"

June looked around warily. "No one has seen my mother."

Typhon looked confused.

She explained how she had been to visit twice in a week and she hadn't been there, and Henry had not seen her here in multiple. She didn't mention Asclepius, not even sure how to explain the strange part-god-part-snake person. Typhon's face went grim and he nodded. Reaching down to hold June's hand, they walked together up to Helen's porch.

21

June and Typhon stood, frozen from shock, in front of her childhood home.

The front yard was nearly completely dead, more so than was normal for this time of year. The flowers that lined the walk clearly hadn't been watered in recent days, and the mailbox was stuffed so full it was dropping letters on the ground. June racked her brain, thinking back to when she'd seen her mother last. The days had blurred together and it took a moment to realize that it really had been weeks before, and she wondered how fast things died when they weren't watered.

June reached out a hand and pushed the gate, and the hinges creaked loudly, cutting through the still air. Mother hated that sharp sound and usually kept the gate well-greased.

Typhon and June glanced at each other. He gave her a questioning look and she shook her head. He whispered, "Good luck," and reached a hand to the sky. He seemed to intertwine his fingers with a light breeze and was pulled up into nothingness in a moment.

June stepped forward, forcing herself to swallow hard and keep moving. The house was dark, and piles of leaves took up most of the porch—another strange thing. June continued up the steps, pausing to knock. No answer. She tried again, louder this time, and waited, ear pressed to the door.

There was no movement on the other side. She tried the door handle and was surprised to find it unlocked. Her mother would never leave it that way. She took a tentative step into the entryway as the hinges groaned and the door swung open. She jumped when the handle tapped the wall behind it, and she laughed nervously as she walked into the house.

"Hello?" Her voice echoed down the hall. No response came.

The sudden terrible image of her mother dead on the floor flashed through her mind. She tried to shake it out, and blood spattered around the picture before it faded. Nausea rose up and she swallowed hard, trying to ignore her nerves running wild.

She froze when she stepped into the living room. The blanket and small pillows that normally decorated the couch were thrown across the floor. The inner curtain on the massive window facing the road was torn. The corner of the rug was turned up, and her mother's favorite family portrait was askew on the wall. Knickknacks that normally lined the fireplace mantle and small side table were knocked aside as well. June sucked a breath in and went to the kitchen, where she found a similar state.

Dishes were shattered on the floor. Cabinets were flung open. The hand towel was in the sink. As she slowly walked through the kitchen, she was relieved to find there was no blood, although there had clearly been a struggle. The dining room was untouched, save for a chair that her mother must have been sitting in. June carefully tucked it into place and ventured back down the hall toward her parents' bedroom.

Before she could open the door, a rustling sound filled the hallway and she spun quickly, ready to swing at whoever was there. She let out a loud sigh of relief as Asclepius materialized in front of her. The relief turned to annoyance as she remembered their last encounter, and then morphed into irritation as she noticed the wide grin on their face.

"What?" she hissed.

The god tsked at her before stepping away from the wall they leaned on. "Is that any way to greet an old friend?" They moved to walk past her and into the bedroom, but she stepped into their path.

"I wouldn't call you a friend."

They raised their hands in mock surrender and stepped back, allowing June to stick her head through the doorway. Everything was normal in there.

"Would I be a friend if I knew what happened?"

June whipped her head around and glared at them. "What do you know, snake?" She laced her words with as much venom as she could muster.

"Oh, nothing. It was purely rhetorical." The ice in her eyes did not thaw as the god walked into Helen's room and stepped up to the wide vanity opposite the bed, tracing the hand-carved edge with a gold-tipped nail. They turned and smirked at June.

"I don't know what happened in here *per se*."

June forgot their size difference in an instant and descended on the god, reaching up to grab the collar of their suit and yanking them down to eye level. Asclepius quickly transformed, but that forced June's hand to tighten around their neck. Their slitted eyes bulged and they popped back into human form, now bent at an awkward angle and nearly nose-to-nose with June.

"What . . . happened . . . snake?" She was seething, rage making her voice shake, and she squeezed Asclepius tighter and tighter. Finally, they threw up their hands again, coughing and sputtering when she released them.

"Okay, okay." They breathed unsteadily. "Yeesh, you're stronger than you look."

June fixed them with a glare, and they stepped back.

"Someone took her."

"Who?" June demanded.

Asclepius raised their hands further, wincing at the tone in her voice. "I can't tell you exactly, but . . ." They chuckled. "Navy suit."

Confusion bled into June's anger and she continued glowering at the snake-turned-person.

They laughed again, a bit louder. "She didn't go down easy."

June thought they sounded a bit deranged for a moment, and she raised a brow at them.

"From what I could hear," they added hastily, shrugging. "Guess we know where you get that fire from."

June promptly turned and stormed from the room. Asclepius ran after her to yell, "Wait, where are you going?"

She ignored them and kept walking, leaving the house and breaking into a run down the street. She had a feeling that she knew exactly who those suits were. How dare Poseidon come for Helen after what he already did to her! Tears stung her eyes as she ran, heart pumping hard and blood rushing in her ears. How could he think he could get away with this!

She had only considered revenge on him for a moment before, but now, this was war. She was going to get her mother back, and get rid of him, if it was the last thing she did. How could she let herself fall back into routine after the attack confused her? She'd felt so powerful, using what was given to her. Almost untouchable. She'd completely forgotten about the debt that needed to be paid and the reason she was selling dead men.

June ran as fast as she could back to the café around the corner. She had to make a plan. Right now. She was going to fix this. She'd use her power against Poseidon, or figure something else out.

She ignored the strange look from the barista as she flopped back into her chair. She breathed heavily and tried to slow her heartbeat. She flipped open her book and wrote:
First, find Don.
Second, where is Mom?
Third,
Her furious scribbles were stopped by a familiar voice. "Here you are again!"

She rolled her eyes and looked up to see Henry standing in front of her table. "Are you still following me, Mr. Chekov?"

Henry's face fell for a moment and he regained his composure quickly. "It's really just Henry, please. And, actually, I was just here for a coffee. What's going on?"

June rolled her eyes again, more obviously this time. She did not have the patience to deal with this man's nonsense right now. "Nothing, actually. I have some work to do."

Henry nodded and smiled. "I'll leave you to it then."

June waved vaguely, and as Henry stepped away to sit at a table nearby, the barista set a cup of coffee in front of June. The smell wafted up and forced its way into her nose, and before she could register what was happening, she doubled over in a wave of dizziness and nausea. A groan escaped her lips as she hunched and ran for the restroom, swinging the door open wide and barely making it to the toilet before the contents of her stomach came up.

She gripped the cold porcelain and vomited until nothing but acid remained. Resting her forehead against the cold bowl, she felt a hand on the back of her neck, and Henry's voice pierced through her fog. "June! Are you okay?"

Tears prickled behind her eyelids as she squeezed them shut, and she leaned back into Henry, who quickly lifted her up and helped her out of the restroom.

He guided her from the café to a black car outside. Through her blurred vision and dizzy spell, she noticed it was the same black car that had followed her.

He helped her into the passenger seat, careful to make sure she was upright before closing the door. He climbed into his own seat, glancing at her with obvious concern, before reversing and tearing to the hospital.

June barely remained conscious for the drive, alternating between crying and becoming too dizzy to hold her head up.

Through her daze, June was vaguely aware of Henry's hands on her arms, holding her up as he guided her into the hospital. He said something to a nurse, and she was whisked into a small room. The smell of chemicals filled the air and helped clear her head, and she looked around to try and get a bearing on where she was. She didn't remember lying down, but a thin bed with a metal frame and stark white sheets was underneath her. A flimsy chair sat next to her, with a cloth-covered table and mirror across the room. Her skin was clammy, and as she raised a hand to wipe sweat from her forehead, it shook.

Henry paced nearby, concern clear. Finally, a doctor appeared in the doorway. June couldn't make out their conversation as they carried on in hushed whispers, but by the time the doctor disappeared again, she was starting to feel more normal.

Henry crouched by the bed and reached out to hold her hand, stopping as she looked at him and pulling back after grazing her fingertips.

"How do you feel?" he whispered.

"I think I'm okay." Her throat was sore from vomiting and her voice sounded hoarse. Henry did not look convinced, and he gazed at her with something unrecognizable in his eyes. Before he could say anything else, a nurse shooed him out to make room for the medical staff. A doctor walked in carrying a tray with all sorts of tools and cups, and after he placed it down, he asked June some questions and poked and prodded her. June did as she was instructed, and as she returned to the bed, another wave of nausea washed over her. Henry returned as soon as there was space in the room, and he held a tin bucket for her as she leaned over the edge of the hospital bed and retched. Thankfully, nothing came up and the feeling subsided quickly.

The pair sat together in the hospital room for a couple of hours before the doctor came back to dismiss them. He promised he would be in touch soon with an answer to her problem.

As Henry helped June climb into his car, she suddenly turned to him. "You were the one following me!"

He looked taken aback and looked around as if searching for help before responding. "I told you that," he said slowly.

June, dumbstruck, leaned back in her seat and let him close the door.

He had, indeed, but for some reason, she hadn't connected the car with Henry. That meant that he was there from the beginning, when Typhon helped her haul the man from the park.

Henry took his place at the steering wheel and threw a glance her way before starting the car and driving back to June's apartment.

They were silent the entire way, until he parked in front of the gallery and moved to get out and open her door. She shook her head. "It's okay, I can do it."

She climbed out of the car and hesitated before saying, "Thank you," and slamming the door. She went upstairs quickly, anxious to get into bed. It was only late afternoon, but her body felt heavy, and her mind even more so. She thought that perhaps some sleep would settle her nerves and sickness. Then she could find her mom and deal with Poseidon.

22

Bright light blinded June as she squinted against it. It took a moment for her eyes to adjust before she realized that it was actually the sun shining down on her. She looked down and examined herself. She was confused, as she could swear that she had just been in bed.

She was dressed in a strange white robe, tied in place at her waist with a golden braid. The skin on her arms looked fresh, glowing even, and there was no trace of the nervous sweat that had been coating her body earlier. In fact, she felt amazing. No knots in her stomach, no anxiety riddling her brain. She looked around and was surprised to see that she was standing in a large, marble room. Gray veins formed intricate patterns in the glossy white surface, and columns lined the room. She raised her hand to shield her eyes from the sun and looked up to see a gilded ceiling, with a hole cut in to let the light. It shined directly where she stood.

She stepped to the side and looked around again.

"Welcome, young one." A voice behind her echoed around the chamber, and she spun to see a handsome man step forward. He looked old enough to be her grandfather. She felt calm, and she smiled at him.

"Hello," she said pleasantly, her voice coming out easily.

The man walked toward her and held out his arm, which she graciously accepted. They walked around the room slowly, her hand on his upper arm. As they walked in silence, she studied him. He was the same height and build as Poseidon, but he appeared much older. With a grizzly gray beard sticking out at odd angles, and short graying hair to match, his eyes were the shade of rain clouds before they threw a storm down over the city, and they seemed to swirl like clouds too.

As they approached a doorway, the sound of a waterfall filled the air around them, and they stepped out onto soft green grass. Butterflies and other insects flitted here and there, and the sun shone brightly against a bright blue sky.

"Where are we?" June finally asked.

The man simply smiled and continued leading the way over a small wooden footbridge. He suddenly looked at her as if he'd remembered something. "Congratulations on your exciting news!"

Puzzled, June stopped. "What do you mean?"

The man with the gray eyes looked down at her stomach. She looked down, and, suddenly, where there was nothing before, June now held a bulging bump. It was as if she had become eight months pregnant in a matter of seconds. Horrified, she looked back up to ask what happened, but the man was gone.

The bright colors around her faded, and a loud booming sound echoed from the horizon while the grass and water around her melted from under her feet. She began to fall, her scream caught on the wind that blew up past her body as she fell through dark space. She wasn't sure if she was screaming because of the pregnancy or because of the fear of going splat on the ground, but it was torn from her by the torrential wind anyway.

Thick black streams of stars passed her in a blur, caressing bits of her free-falling body as she was thrown down. She twisted and turned through tendrils of ink until she could see herself falling toward the slowly spinning Earth. It came closer and closer until she could almost make out the buildings of New York. She squeezed her eyes shut, bracing for impact.

23

"June!" A loud banging sound woke June with a start, and she quickly sat up, her dream fading fast. She tore back her blankets and looked at her stomach, sighing with relief at the lack of a bump. She crawled out of bed and slid her feet into slippers before running downstairs.

Henry called her name twice more from behind the door before she reached it and swung it wide open. He nearly tripped over the entry and grabbed the doorframe to balance himself. June laughed and Henry started, seeming surprised before smiling.

"How are you doing?"

June stepped back to let Henry in as she said, "Good, I think. Thank you."

Henry smiled before walking into the kitchen and standing awkwardly by the counter. June stopped a few feet away from him and waited. Finally, he cleared his throat and asked, "Would you like to go get dinner? With me, I mean."

She cocked her head and looked at him. As her gaze wandered up and down his body, she noticed he was wearing the same mismatched suit that seemed to be his trademark. When she looked him in the eyes, a blush crept up into her cheeks. He was looking at her intensely, his brown eyes radiating warmth and a sense of innocence.

"What do you mean?" she asked.

He cleared his throat again, beginning to look nervous. "I'd like to take you on a date, if you're feeling up to it."

June faltered. She had never been on a date.

He must have mistaken the look on her face for hesitation, instead of the confusion she really felt at being asked out, and he began to ramble. "I couldn't help but see your notebook the other day, and it seems like you might be having a hard time. I'd like to help. I know a Don . . ." He trailed off as her expression went dark. "I'm sorry," he whispered.

She shook her head. "I'm not mad at you. There's . . . a lot going on."

Henry nodded. "Well, would you like to go get dinner? We can talk about it."

June crossed her arms. "Yeah, that sounds nice. I could use some help. Although, it's against my better judgment to confide in the person investigating my family." She held up a finger. "And, it's not a date. Just dinner to talk about the mess I'm in."

Henry smiled, nearly beaming, and nodded. June motioned to the dining table and asked him to wait while she got cleaned up. He obeyed. As she walked upstairs to her room, it dawned on her that she hadn't been wearing her sunglasses. She smiled to herself.

By the time she came back downstairs, the sun had set. June's stomach grumbled as they set out and walked to an Italian restaurant two blocks away.

She noticed that Henry was careful to walk between her and the road, switching sides when they crossed the street. She smiled at that, and again when they reached the restaurant and he ran ahead to hold the door open for her.

They were seated quickly, and Henry broke the silence first to ask, "What's going on?"

June took a sip of water, then rested her head in her hands. "My mother is missing."

Henry choked on his drink. He coughed and cleared his throat before leaning forward. "Missing? What do you mean? I mean, I saw 'Find Mom' written in your book, but I didn't think that was meant so literally."

June lifted her head and forced a smile on her face. "Are we friends, Henry? Or is this you investigating?"

Henry picked at a hangnail, clearly uncomfortable. "I thought we could be friends . . ." He trailed off and met her gaze.

Unsure what to say, June nodded.

They were quiet for a long moment before she began again. "A few weeks back, I was attacked at work—by Don. It had something to do with my father owing a debt." She waved her hand dismissively at Henry's concerned expression. "Anyway, I haven't seen my mother for a week. I initially thought that she had gone on a holiday, but then you said this morning that she wasn't home even before a week ago." She paused and waited for Henry to nod, then continued. "I went to see if she was there immediately after that, but when I walked into her house, she was gone, and it seems she was taken against her will."

Henry breathed sharply and June began to tear up as she shared the details of her mother's belongings being knocked down and everything being out of place.

The pair went quiet as the waiter set silverware in front of them, and Henry leaned back over the table once he was gone. "Do you think they were looking for something?"

June shook her head slowly. "I'm not sure. I haven't had much time to think about it."

Henry leaned back and chewed his lip, seeming lost in thought as the waiter returned and served them each a large plate of pasta. June's stomach turned at the sight of the noodles, as it reminded her of snakes. She forced herself to take a bite, then another. She had to eat, or vomiting would be the least of her worries.

"I wonder if Don took her to try and lure you in."

June startled at Henry's statement and laughed. "Why would he do that? I'm not anyone special."

Henry shrugged. "Think about it. He came to collect a debt from you, right? If that didn't make your father pay, then what next but to take his wife? Still no answer from your father? Leave a clear path of destruction and wait for the mouse to chase the cheese. The mouse here being you, of course. Then Don could use you and your mother to get to William."

June chewed as she pondered. She swallowed hard, and the bite of pasta felt like lead as it slid down her throat. "Maybe you're right."

Henry looked at her with an almost frightened expression. "My old boss was a man named Don Whittaker."

June went pale.

"Well, unofficial boss of my boss. I'm pretty sure he owns the department, even though it shouldn't work like that. But he would come into work and do terrible things to the lower officers. I watched him shoot a man once."

June's hand trembled as she tried to take a drink, her throat suddenly dry. How could her father become so indebted to the bank that the owner would come looking for her? Or did running the mob come first and owning the bank was simply a byproduct of that role?

Henry grinned his goofy grin, all air of terror gone. "It can't possibly be the same Don, right?" His face dropped as he noticed the look on June's face, and he looked down at his plate. "I don't think I'm hungry anymore."

June nodded her agreement, and they sat in silence until the server came and took their nearly full plates. He crinkled his nose up, as if they were some strange creatures. June tried her best to smile at him, but she was shaken to her core. Don's reach was far too large, and she couldn't understand how. How could one man be entrenched in the police department and be collecting on the smaller debts he's owed? Oh, right, a god could.

Henry led them out of the restaurant, once again holding the door open for June. They stood outside together, backs lit by the warm light cast out of the windows behind them, and he turned to her. "Maybe you should go to his work. Your father's, I mean. They may have an idea of where his money was going. It was the plant, right?"

June stopped and nodded, anxiety sending a chill up her spine.

"They won't let just anyone in. I'll sneak in and borrow a uniform for you." He smiled, and June thanked him.

"But why would you help?" she asked.

He shrugged. "You seem nice, and police are meant to help. I'll go tomorrow." Henry reached out a hand to squeeze hers. "I'll swing by in the morn—" His sentence was cut off and hand torn away from June's as a large mass threw June backward and jumped on him.

"Henry!" it squealed.

Wind knocked out of her, June straightened and rebalanced herself before looking at the woman now standing with her arms wrapped tightly around Henry's neck. He had crimson cheeks and held one hand out, hovering over the woman's back, as if he was unsure whether or not to return the embrace.

June cleared her throat and spoke. "Hello . . ." She trailed off as the woman turned. She wore a floor-length velvet gown with matching gloves and a long fur-lined coat. Her hair was curled in an updo, and when June saw her face, she laughed in disbelief. "Sarah?"

Henry looked confused. "This is Eris," he said blankly.

The woman laughed, looking back and forth between them. "Oh goody, my boyfriend and my hero in the same place."

June swore the confusion on Henry's face matched her own, but she blurted out, "Boyfriend?" at the same moment Henry asked, "Hero?" They exchanged a look that further deepened the red in Henry's face.

June stepped forward to address Sarah, who still had an arm around Henry's waist. "I thought your name was Sarah. That's what you told me in the park."

The other woman shrugged. "Sorry, I lied."

June began to feel irritated as she watched Eris reach up and try to kiss Henry, who turned his face away. June cleared her throat loudly, and Eris finally let go of the chokehold she had Henry in and spun, planting her hands on her hips. "Yes?" She raised an eyebrow, as if June was intruding on her night, and June swore a bit of electricity crackled between them. It wasn't nearly as strong as Asclepius' aura, but it was something.

June's anger flushed her skin. "Henry would not have asked me on a date if he was seeing someone."

A look of pure rage crossed Eris' face before she smoothed the front of her dress, shook her head once, as if ridding her ear of water, and smirked. "I'm sure he didn't think it was a date. We were just out together the other night, after all."

June looked at Henry for some explanation, but he just blushed darker and didn't even open his mouth to try and deny anything. She glared at Eris' back as the woman snaked her arms back around Henry's neck and leaned up. June didn't stay to watch the kiss she planted, instead turning and stomping down the road toward home.

24

Typhon floated outside June's window, watching sadly as she slammed her kettle on the stove. It had been days since he had spoken to her. He felt bad watching from a distance, and he felt he should check in but wasn't sure how to. In the eighteen years since they'd met, they had never fought. And after she didn't ask him to go to her mother's house with her, he was worried that she hated him. Mortals were so complicated sometimes. Perhaps that was him and his lack of interaction over the years.

June yanked a mug from the cabinet and put it on the counter with so much force that the handle broke off. Typhon continued to watch. She set the handle down and braced her hands on the counter, leaning down and sighing loudly. A moment later, she looked down and placed a hand on her stomach, turning this way and that.

Oh no, he thought. He shoved the window open and blew in, stepping into his solid form next to the dining table.

June turned and stared at him. He took his hat off and stared back awkwardly. They stood like that for a long minute, with Typhon trying to figure out what to say.

Suddenly, she bounded across the room. Throwing her arms around him, she began crying. "Oh, Ty, I'm so glad you're here!"

Typhon smiled and returned the warm embrace, relieved that she hadn't held a grudge.

When June stepped back, she asked, "Tea?"

"Please." Ty sat at the table and waited while June poured a cup for each of them. "What's going on, June-bee?"

June grimaced and wrapped her hands around her mug, watching the steam rise for a moment before choking out, "Mom's missing."

Ty nodded empathetically and reached across the table to pat her hand.

"Plus Henry has a girl, and I only found out after he asked me on a date."

Ty's face screwed up. "Who's Henry again?"

"Well, he started as the officer investigating Dad's disappearance, but I think I was hoping for more than a professional relationship." June smiled and told him about the rest of their interactions.

He nodded when she finished. He'd known all this already, but he didn't want her to think that he'd infringed on her privacy. "Who's the floozy?"

June laughed. "Some woman named Eris, who I thought was named Sarah, who I saved in the park."

Typhon snapped his fingers. "Ah! I remember her. Although, Eris is not a mortal name."

June cocked her head, confused.

"There's an Eris on Olympus—or used to be. I've only ever heard of the one. She's the goddess of chaos, and an absolute irritant."

June nodded slowly. "I feel bad. I left before he could explain anything, but I don't know if even he would know."

Typhon shook his head. "Don't worry. He'll come back."

June thanked him and sipped her tea. He leaned back, remembering his own time with Eris. She was truly a man-eater. About a hundred years ago, she had lured him in, moved too fast too quickly, and then set up an awful scene for him to walk in on. After a terrible natural disaster, he came back to his room on Olympus to find her wrapped up tightly with his mother, Gaia. He shuddered at the memory. Hopefully she'd settled down in the century that she'd been on Earth.

"So what's the plan?" he asked.

June's head snapped up and she looked confused.

"For your mom."

"Oh. Henry suggested I go to Dad's old work. He said he'd bring by a borrowed uniform in the morning." Worry creased her brow and Typhon offered a reassuring smile.

They sat together and drank their tea in silence, before Typhon set his mug down and clasped his hands, a serious look on his face. June mimicked him and smiled when he rolled his eyes.

"What's going on there?" he said quietly, pointing at her stomach. Her face fell, and it hit Typhon. "Are you . . .?" he whispered.

She nodded. "I think so. I think Poseidon got me pregnant." Tears glistened in her eyes, and the pain etched into her features was obvious. Typhon swore. That no-good, piece-of-crap god! He kept doing this, and he wouldn't be stopped.

Typhon kept his opinions to himself and asked what she would do.

"There's not much I can do," she said, sadness clear in her voice.

She was such a strong girl, and he knew she would be okay, but he was hurting for her. He nodded absentmindedly. They sat together, not speaking for a long time. Typhon finally set down his mug and rose to leave, making sure to give June a tight hug before drifting out of the window. He carried a few stray leaves up, rising until June's apartment was just a speck below him.

25

A bleary morning dawned after a sleepless night. Dreams haunted her — terrible dreams of Eris strutting up to Henry and throwing her dress around him, making it turn into vines to wrap around his legs like tree roots. She woke with crusted eyes and a dull thud behind her left eye.

She sat up in bed and scrubbed her face with her hands, wiping the sleep from her eyes, and looked out the window. The sky was gray, and the sun had barely started to rise. As she stood and pulled a robe on, the last image of Eris inhaling Henry's soul through his mouth faded, and she meandered downstairs.

She pulled a small piece of ginger from the fridge and chewed it slowly, eyeing the front page of yesterday's paper on the counter. "Yanks lose six to one in seventy-two minutes." She rolled her eyes and turned the page. Really, who cared?

As she scanned the second page and swallowed her last bite of ginger, hoping it would settle her stomach, a knock sounded from the door.

When she opened it, she was shocked to see Henry in a state of disarray. She gasped as she looked at his face. One of his eyes was swollen shut and colored a sickening shade of violet. His lip was missing a slice from it, and blood trickled from his right ear. His typical white button-down was torn at the collar, and his coat was nowhere in sight, although he held a tight bundle of dirty blue cloth in one hand.

"What happened?" June asked as she ushered him in.

He grinned sheepishly and shrugged. "Lovers' quarrel?" he offered, as he stepped past her and went to the dining room.

June snorted a laugh and stopped in front of him. She looked him up and down once more before pointing at a chair and saying, "Sit." He obeyed, and she got to work making him breakfast. She grabbed some eggs from the basket on her counter and vegetables from the fridge, and as she chopped mushrooms, Henry explained.

"I went to the plant like we discussed, but for some reason, Eris was there. She beat the living hell out of me for embarrassing her." He rubbed the back of his neck and looked up at June, before placing his hands on his knees, palms up. "I'm sorry."

She stiffened. "What for?" She tried her best to sound as if nothing had happened. She carefully cracked two eggs in the pan and added a handful of mushrooms and tomatoes before taking a spatula and breaking the yolks open, perhaps a bit forcefully.

"I should have told you. I did take her on a date, but it was over a week ago and I hadn't seen her since. I didn't think anything of it because we weren't really seeing each other."

June nodded, tension in her shoulders giving way to relief. She hadn't realized how interested she was in Henry before, and the thought of him involved in this chaos with the gods, or the goddess of chaos herself, made her upset.

She mentally kicked herself for caring so much when they had only properly met a few days before. She flipped the omelet out of the pan and took the plate to Henry, stopping a foot away. He still looked apologetic, almost as if he was waiting for her to yell or hit him. She set the plate down gently and squeezed his shoulder.

"It's okay." She caught a glimpse of a smile breaking across Henry's face as she moved to serve herself.

He watched with awe in his face as she carefully mixed her own breakfast in the pan, a quiet tune escaping her lips. She pretended she couldn't see how he was looking at her, and she did her best to ignore the strange mix of emotions bubbling in her chest. He didn't touch his plate until she sat across from him, then they ate in silence, stealing glances at each other.

Once their plates were clear, June smiled at Henry, trying to keep the butterflies down that had joined her breakfast.

"Well, I guess I better go to work," she finally said, breaking the strange silence. Henry grinned and she laughed before he pulled a crumpled ball of fabric from the seat next to him and shook it out to reveal a factory jumpsuit. The surname "Williams" was stitched on the front, and June gave him a wry smile as she read that.

She went upstairs and dressed quickly, then donned one of Ty's driver's caps that he'd given her as a child, careful to tuck her stray curls up into it. She pulled her sunglasses on and slid her feet into an old pair of her father's work boots. They were at least four sizes too big, but she hoped that would lend to her looking like a man.

After she took a few steps, she grimaced and slid her feet back out, taking a moment to hunt down spare stockings from around the room. She stuffed them into the toes of each boot and tried again. They weren't so clunky and loose now.

When she returned downstairs, Henry was gone, but she was pleasantly surprised to see that he had cleaned up the breakfast dishes and put away the leftover food. She couldn't stop to appreciate the gesture for too long, though, as she had to move quickly.

She left the house and strode down the sidewalk with purpose, heading for the plant that her father worked at. Thankfully, it was only on the other side of Central Park, about twenty minutes. She swallowed back a bit of nausea as she went, and it got her thinking. What was she to do with a baby? Thinking of the prospect of raising a child alone made her feel younger than ever. As she passed the café where she first met Henry, her thoughts turned to him. She hadn't considered him to have potential for a relationship when they had met a couple days ago, but the more they were seemingly forced together, the more she enjoyed his company. She wondered if he felt the same. She hoped it wasn't superficial and just a way to get answers on her father.

As she passed the park, a familiar slithering sound caught her attention. She rolled her eyes as a large snake began to weave next to her. Its scales were pitch black without the sunlight to change them. "Really, Pius? Not now."

Asclepius sprang up next to her and scrunched their flat nose at her. "Did you really just nickname a god, girl?"

She shrugged and kept walking, speeding up slightly to try and lose her new companion. Really, she didn't give a single crap if they liked the name or not.

They jogged the few steps it took to catch up, then spun around to walk backward in front of her. "Where are you going?"

June sniffed. "None of your business, snake."

They held up their arms. "Okay, I know I haven't been the nicest, and I'm sorry." Their gold-tinted lips spread into a grin. "There are bigger things at play here, though."

June stopped and narrowed her eyes. "What do you mean?"

Pius' eyes twinkled. "You tell me yours, I'll tell you mine."

June sighed and began her walk again, and Asclepius fell into stride next to her. It wasn't as if she had an abundance of gods to get information from. Even if Asclepius was a snake, in more ways than one, if they could give her some inkling as to what was going on outside of her small world . . . maybe it would give her a leg up over Poseidon.

"I'm going to the factory my father worked at. I'm going to see if his boss knows anything further about the debt he owes." She turned to demand an answer to her question, but she was alone again. She shook her head and muttered, "Gods," before turning a corner and coming to a halt in front of a large, gray-washed building. The length of six generously sized houses, and twice as tall, it towered over her, casting a massive, ominous shadow. She looked around and spotted a large group of men heading to the entrance of the lot. She jogged to catch up, falling into step behind them.

She managed to slip in with the group undetected, and she tried to keep her head down as she looked around for a manager's office or someone not in a jumpsuit. A man in front of her headed for the back of the building, and she followed, trying to ignore the large machines. She wasn't sure exactly what this plant was even for, but it was huge—and smelly.

She stuck to the man's shadow until he turned right, grabbing a stack of papers from the wall in front of him and heading for another group of workers ten feet away. She looked up and was shocked to see a door in front of her with the word *Office* written on it. She tried the handle, and it opened. As she began to walk in, a man yelled from her left. "Hey!" She froze. "No eyewear aside from safety glasses." June dropped her voice as low as it could go and called back, "Sorry," before ducking into the office and exhaling loudly. That was almost too easy.

With her hand still on the door handle, she heard someone clear their throat behind her, and she steeled herself, ready to face the manager. As she turned, the pair of blue eyes looking back at her sent a cold shock down her spine. "Eris?"

Her cheeks heated and she balled her hands into fists as Eris smiled wryly. The goddess motioned to the chair in front of her. "Please sit, June."

June moved to the chair, trying to hide her confusion while not breaking eye contact. "I'm here about my father." Her tone was even but her heart was hammering at her ribs.

Eris sighed and moved the stack of papers in front of her. All traces of the cynicism and loathing in her expression faded. June looked her up and down, surprised to see that she was wearing a suit. It looked like a man's typical work suit, but it had been tailored to accent her narrow waist. She looked down and saw a name plate that read, "Sarah Johnson, CEO."

June hid her discomfort as well as she could and waited for Eris to speak.

"I knew you'd be here sooner or later since your father disappeared. We've all been wondering where he's gone to, you know." She looked June in the eye and cocked her head.

June cleared her throat. "He's become indisposed. What are you doing here, Eris? First, you're in a park being attacked, then, seemingly attacking my date. Now you run an entirely male-staffed plant?"

Eris shrugged. "I'm a woman of many talents."

June stood up in a rush and slammed her hands on the desk. "Cut the nonsense. I know exactly who you are, and you're going to tell me what my father did to cause Poseidon to seek me out. You were his boss. He spent most of his time here. What happened?" She gritted her teeth, and Eris crossed her arms and raised an eyebrow, nodding at the chair. June breathed in heavily to try and calm the rage boiling in her chest before resuming her seat.

"I can't tell you the extent of your father's issues. I don't even know. I was his boss before getting involved in your life. But I can tell you two things. First, he hasn't been here in a long time." June scoffed. "Second, he took out a lot of advances before leaving with no notice. He owes me a lot of hours, or a lot of money. Either of which I would be happy to collect on." Eris sighed at June's glare again, muttering, "I have a boss to report to too."

June laughed and leaned forward. "Oh yeah? Who is that?"

Eris pointed out of the office window then, and June turned, her breath catching in her throat. A cold sinking feeling took over as she watched three men in navy suits walk through the front door. Terror took over June. "How much money?"

"A lot."

June nodded. She watched them stop, and the middle man asked a worker something, to which the worker responded by pointing to the window June now peered through. She spun and faced Eris. "Why are they here?"

She spoke softly, voice barely above a whisper. "Their boss is my boss, dear. He's the boss of New York."

Understanding dawned on June then. Typhon had been serious when he said that Poseidon was set to take over everything. There was no denying that her fate was now intertwined with a truly awful person. He deserved everything she planned to bring to him.

"Eris, on the topic of honesty, where can I find him?" She glanced through the window to see the suits getting closer, and her legs shook.

Eris gave another nonchalant shrug. "I'm not sure." June glared at her until she finally rolled her eyes and said, "There's a gentleman's club. Middle of downtown. Try there. I'll see if I can find someone to meet you."

"Thanks." June breathed hard before standing. She started to move to the door, but Eris stopped her, steely eyes holding June's green ones.

"Understand something. This is way bigger than you. And I hold loyalties to no individual. Next time we meet, I may not be so accommodating. We are all just pawns trying to stay on the board."

June nodded, the hairs on her neck raising. "I wouldn't fault you. You're the goddess of chaos, after all," she said stiffly, and a Cheshire grin stretched across Eris' face.

June went to the door and realized that she couldn't run past the suits without getting caught.

Her heart pounded as they were stopped by the man with the papers just twenty feet away.

Eris cleared her throat and June whirled to see her pointing at a door to the side of the office. June thanked her again and burst through it into bright sun shining onto a small parking lot. Sunshine after a gray morning had to be a good omen, she thought.

She began running across the parking lot, her oversized boots clumping loudly with each step. Dizziness started to take over her again and she silently begged it to stop. She couldn't get sick right now. As she threw herself through a thin gap in the fence to the street beyond, a deep voice yelled, "Hey!" from the office door. She didn't stop.

June ran as hard as she could the entire way home. She thought she heard Typhon's voice on the breeze at one point, but she ignored it.

When she finally reached her apartment, she threw the door open and slammed it behind her, flicking the lock before gasping and trying to catch her breath. She grabbed at the stitch in her side and walked to the kitchen, shocked to see Henry sitting there. He jumped up and set his newspaper down, hurrying around to pull her chair out.

"What are you doing here?" she asked coolly. She wasn't sure about the ins and outs of dating a man, but she was quite sure that it wasn't normal for them to hang around or sneak into a woman's house.

Henry froze and looked at her, seeming confused. "I thought you would want a friend after the trip." He twisted his fingers together and looked at the ground. "Plus I thought being here might make up for the miscommunication."

June's back tensed as she sized him up. He had clearly cleaned himself up since the morning, wearing his signature mismatched suit and navy coat. His lip and eye were still swollen but looked much better. He busied himself making tea while she leaned back in the chair and kicked off the ridiculous boots, gulping air and trying to swallow back the bile that rose in the back of her throat.

Henry handed her a hot cup, and she took it gratefully while he slid into the seat across from her. Her mind raced, trying to think of how she was going to let Henry in on what was going on without giving too much away. She liked him, but she wasn't sure she could trust him. She'd have to gauge his reaction as they went.

He looked at her as the silence stretched between them. She finally blurted out, "Eris was his boss," before taking a long draw from her mug. Henry's jaw dropped and June nodded at his shocked expression. "And Don is her boss."

Henry carefully set down his cup with shaking hands. "My Don?"

"Our Don," she corrected.

"That's who sent me to ask questions, you know."

June groaned. "I knew, but it didn't click. He's the reason I—" She stopped herself. "Never mind."

Henry gave her a sad look. "We will figure this out together."

"We? This is on me, Henry. My mother was the one taken. My father was the one that put us in debt."

"I can help!" he exclaimed. "We'll figure it out together."

June leaned in, raising an eyebrow at him. "Why do you want to help, Henry? What do you have to gain aside from information to feed back to Don?"

Henry shook his head. "I'm not going to tell him anything, at least nothing like this. You're just trying to figure out what's been hidden from you to better pay back the debt. The extent of my job regarding you was to get answers about William's whereabouts." He leaned forward, his fingers brushing against her knuckles. "And, frankly, I like you."

June smiled and thanked him, before pulling her notebook out from the shelf next to them. "If you want to help, there are some things you need to know. And—" she raised a finger "—you can't just bust into ladies' homes anymore."

Henry grinned sheepishly and nodded.

As if on cue, a gust of wind blew the window open. Three stray leaves landed on the kitchen floor, and June clasped her hands, looking at Henry intently.

"Henry, what do you know about the gods?"

He looked a bit shaken. "I'm not sure. I guess I never really believed they existed."

June breathed deeply before speaking, worried he might think she was crazy and get up and run away. "This might sound crazy, but bear with me. We don't have the luxury of time to ease you in. What if I told you that they walked among us and that there was more to the world than you could believe?"

Henry gripped his cup tightly enough to turn his knuckles white. "I'm not sure." He seemed anxious, and June smiled to reassure him.

"All right, Ty," she announced, facing the empty kitchen. Henry blinked at her, and then suddenly, the breeze swirled again and Typhon stood where the leaves were before. His tan suit was crisp and new-looking, and he'd changed out the brown driver's cap for a tweed one. June saw Henry jump back in his chair, and she tried not to smile. Typhon inclined his head toward Henry and popped back up with a smile, walking up with his hand outstretched to shake Henry's.

Henry took it, a look of awe and confusion on his face. "H-hi," he stuttered.

Typhon gripped his hand firmly and said hello, before taking a seat between June and Henry.

June cleared her throat. "This is Typhon, Titan God of Wind and Storm . . ." She looked to Ty for confirmation, and he nodded.

Henry's voice shook as he spoke. "It's nice to meet you."

Typhon laughed lightly. "It's okay, I'm not going to smite you. And you can call me Ty. This one has her whole life." He jerked a thumb at June, and she laughed lightly.

Blush creeped in Henry's cheeks and he nodded, as if he was scared to say anything else. June reached across the table and took his hand.

"There's more. Don is actually Poseidon. Typhon could explain it better, but essentially he came down here to wreak havoc and became the 'boss of New York,' as Eris put it." Henry swallowed hard, but she continued. "When he attacked me in that alley, Athena came after and gave me a blessing. Those statues of men downstairs? I created them, but not really. When I look a man in the eye, I can turn him to stone."

Henry jumped up. "You mean to tell me that you could have killed me at any point?"

June smiled sheepishly. "I suppose." She quickly stood as well and held her hands out. "But I didn't, and I don't think I will. I've started getting a handle on it, and I feel safe with you."

Henry ran a hand through his hair and looked around the room as if he was trying to look anywhere but her eyes. June and Typhon exchanged a look but stayed quiet.

After a few minutes of pacing, Henry fell back in his chair, laughing in disbelief. "Remind me never to make you mad."

June laughed and Typhon cleared his throat to bring her back on track.

"Is that why you wear the sunglasses?" Henry asked, words coming slowly.

June nodded. "It helps to have a physical barrier so no accidents happen."

She reached across the table to give Henry's hand a squeeze, and he returned the gesture, still looking uneasy, before she continued. "Back to the point. Don is a dangerous man, and he needs to be dealt with. I'm sure of the fact that he took my mother now, but I've no idea where to find him."

Henry groaned. "How on earth did you ever get involved with him?"

"I didn't!" she exclaimed. "My father did. I know he had a gambling issue, and Eris said he was in debt at work. I'm sure this is all coincidence at this point, but Poseidon is owed big time, and he's trying to collect any way he can. Eris wouldn't tell me how much my father owed, but she said Don visits a club near downtown."

Henry cocked his head. "Spades, maybe?"

June blushed at the idea of Henry visiting a club like that and took a moment to recover.

"That's what I thought, but I'm sure that closed when I was a child."

Henry shrugged, and Typhon chimed in. "You know not everything is as it seems, especially since the prohibition. A lot of, ah, creatures have opened up underground." He shrugged. "It may be worth a shot." He glanced at his watch. "Sorry, kids," he said, standing. "I've got a date with a storm." He winked at June and in a second was gone, twisting on a breeze out the window.

Henry's jaw dropped as he stared after the leaves disappearing in the distance. "Does he do that all the time?"

June laughed at that, a full happy sound, and shook her head. "You'll get used to it."

Henry nodded, roughly scrubbing his hands over his face. June offered him a small smile before picking up a pen and beginning to scribble notes on her blank page.

26

Typhon floated on a wind current outside the dining room window, looking in. He watched as June and Henry leaned in, heads nearly touching, and whispered over a page. They began laughing, and he smiled. A voice below him laughed. He looked down to see Asclepius lounging on a vine, and he said, "Young love, eh?"

Asclepius hissed. "Indeed."

They watched together as June moved to stand beside Henry, placing a hand on his shoulder and reading the paper in front of him, confusion clear on her face. Henry wrapped an arm around her waist and squeezed.

Typhon sighed. "I suppose I'm not needed here anymore. He protects her well, for a human."

Asclepius' tail twitched. "Perhaps you should consider rejoining us in our fight."

Typhon said nothing for a moment. "I never wanted this fight."

Asclepius flicked their tongue and bobbed their head. "None of us did."

"You've clearly chosen your side, though," Typhon snapped, spinning around the vine angrily.

"You have to do what you can to survive."

Silence stretched between them as they watched June and Henry. This was his first real interaction with Asclepius in years, and he was uncomfortable, to put it lightly. It actually took everything in him not to reach out and strangle the snake.

It wasn't so much that Asclepius had ever done him wrong. Typhon just held a general dislike for someone who was supposed to be the god of medicine. They'd become such a, well, snake, over time.

"You know, she's likely the key to ending it all." Asclepius' words interrupted Typhon's thoughts and he spun to look at them.

"No, she couldn't be. She's mortal and wouldn't survive."

Asclepius flicked their tongue. "You never know. She could save us all. Prevent the inevitable war. Speaking of, have you allied? It's really not too late. Sometimes we have to trust those we dislike."

Typhon rolled his eyes. "You know, for an absolute two-faced asshole, you sure do have a lot of wisdom."

Asclepius chuckled, and Typhon turned back to the window and watched for a moment longer before drifting away. Maybe the snake was right. Maybe it was time to find some allies.

His breeze took him up over June's apartment and across town, clear to Eris' house.

27

June and Henry sat together, brainstorming a plan until the sun began to set. Every once in a while, Henry would chime in with a question about the gods, and June would answer to the best of her ability. He seemed as if he was handling all the information well. Perhaps that came with his experience in the field. With a full page of notes written, June glanced out the window and shivered. She pulled a blanket from the shelf and wrapped it around herself, and Henry looked up from his own writing and smiled. "Cold?"

She nodded. "I'm still not used to the early nights."

He checked his watch and gasped. "It's already nearly seven!" He grinned and put his hands flat on the table, leaning forward with a mischievous twinkle in his eye. "Miss Juniper Georgian, may I take you on a dinner date?"

June laughed, not thinking he was serious. He held his gaze on her, and her smile faltered. "We just went out last night."

"You said that wasn't a date."

Butterflies surged up in her stomach and she fiddled with her pen. "I've never been on a real date, Henry. Plus, I feel like I shouldn't be relaxing with my mom gone."

Henry reached across the table and took her hand, wrapping his fingers in hers. "Then let me be the first. I promise it will be fun, and it's healthy to take a break." She finally nodded and Henry smiled. "Go get ready. We'll leave soon."

June gave his fingers a squeeze and went upstairs.

It turned out that getting ready for a real date was stress-inducing, to put it lightly. She couldn't think of a single thing to wear, and she finally opted for a simple light-pink dress that fell below her knees and a dark-navy coat that matched his.

She returned downstairs after almost a half an hour and was greeted by Henry, who was standing awkwardly at the bottom step holding a bouquet of flowers. She smiled and took them graciously, hurrying to find a vase before taking his hand and leaving home.

Henry ran ahead of her to open the passenger side of his car and held out a hand to help her in. They drove in awkward silence, until June finally spoke up as they passed Wall Street. "Where are we going?"

Henry smiled. "It's a surprise." He pulled the car up on the side of the road and moved quickly to help June out, making sure she didn't land too hard on her feet. He held out his arm, and she wrapped her small hand around it, before they fell into step together and ventured down the block. When they approached a corner, June gasped. A tall, gorgeous building stood in front of them. With carved moldings on the outside, the building stood at least six stories high that she could see. She recognized the entrance as Delmonico's, one of the nicest restaurants in the city.

"No, we can't!" she exclaimed, turning to Henry, who gave her a goofy grin.

"We can and will."

They walked through the open door together, still arm in arm, and met a server who took them to a beautifully set table near the back. After they were seated, June leaned in to whisper, "This is so nice!"

Henry laughed and looked over his menu. June set hers down and said, "I can't decide. Will you?"

He nodded, and when the server returned, Henry wrote the order down, careful not to show June. She laughed at him.

When they were alone again, she wasn't sure how to break the silence, so she simply held Henry's hand across the table. He looked at her intently, studying her face, and warmth crept into her cheeks. "You have the most gorgeous eyes, Miss Georgian. Like new flower buds waiting to bloom."

She blushed a deep shade of crimson, stuttering out a thank you.

When the server returned, she was shocked by what was set in front of her. It included a large plate with a glistening piece of steak and helping of mashed carrots, a small dish piled high with caviar, and a platter of breads and oils. She threw her hands up to cover her mouth and gasped. "This is too much!"

Henry smiled. "Nothing is too much for you. You deserve everything good."

June beamed and dug into her dinner.

After a long few minutes of eating, Henry cleared his throat. "So, what's the plan now?"

June set her fork down and gave him a sad look, as the magic of the night dissipated and everything came back. Her mother was missing, her family owed a massive debt, and she was pregnant with the child of a god. What was she supposed to do? She sighed. "I'm not sure. I need to go to Spades. Eris mentioned sending someone."

Henry nodded. "Shall I come with?"

"I appreciate your help, but no. I think I need to do this alone. If he's there, I don't want you to see what might happen." She didn't mention the fact that she didn't fully trust him, and she didn't want to end up with a Henry-sized statue in her gallery if her power went haywire. Gods knew what might happen if someone she liked got involved in a sticky situation.

"This has all been a lot to take in, but I think I sort of always had a feeling." Henry waved his fork a bit. "You know, I was never religious, but my mother regularly prayed to Aphrodite. She would take every chance to keep her marriage to my father strong."

June laughed and nodded. "Yeah, my parents weren't religious at all. Mom tried to educate me on the other Pantheons to keep me unbiased, but I think since Typhon came around, we all had a feeling. At one point my father tried to suggest that maybe there was only one god!" Henry laughed and June smirked. "Imagine, one god doing all that work. Especially now that I know what Typhon does, I couldn't picture him handling everything in this realm."

"I'm glad I know, I think. I almost feel more secure. I wonder if they answer our prayers, though."

June looked away thoughtfully, remembering the night that she thought of Athena and drew an ax. "I think they do to an extent. Athena came to my aid, in her own strange way, after I thought of her."

Henry nodded again, offering a smile before tucking back into his food.

They finished their meal quietly, and as Henry was about to help June from her seat, she suddenly felt sick. "I'm sorry, I'll be right back."

She dashed past the tables next to them and rounded a corner, running straight into someone tall and broad. She stumbled back, keeping her gaze to the floor so as not to hurt an innocent person, and apologized. The familiar smell hit her as the voice reached her ears.

"Well, hello, June." Don's gravel-coated words sent a shock up her spine, and she looked up to meet his eyes.

Anger crashed over her, and she balled her fists, ready to swing as she looked at him. A second passed. Then another. She looked down at his feet, shocked to see that they were still completely normal with no sign of marble.

She looked back up and whispered, "Poseidon."

He grinned at her, almost baring his teeth as he leaned down and whispered in her ear, "How's your mother?"

She tried to shove him back but was instead forced to step back herself. She glared up at him. "What did you do with her?" she demanded.

He chuckled and stepped closer. "Don't worry, she's well taken care of. I wouldn't dare hurt either of you." The color drained in June's face and she tried to stutter out an accusation, but her words failed her. He stepped in again and grabbed her raised hands in his, shoving her against a wall. "Are you here to pay more of your father's debt? You know, he owes me a lot."

She squirmed between him and the solid brick she was pinned against and opened her mouth to scream, but he raised a finger.

"Uh-uh. Can't have that." He leaned down until his face was barely an inch from hers. "Have you moved on from me already, June?" He nodded toward the main dining area of the restaurant. "I see you've seduced one of my employees."

June was suddenly filled with strength from her anger, and she shoved him back. "I haven't seduced anyone, and you were never an interest of mine!" She shoved him back again. "Tell me where my mother is!" She screamed at the top of her lungs, and Poseidon chuckled. She wanted to yank his silver tie down and wrap it around his throat. As if he read her mind, he straightened it and pulled the hem of his jacket down.

"I'm keeping her somewhere William will know to look." June stepped forward, intent on shoving him again, and a wave of nausea suddenly came over her. She froze in her tracks, looked at the ground, and vomited on Don's black loafers. Behind her, Henry skidded to a stop at the end of the hall, and Poseidon's eyes flicked to him for a moment before turning back on June. She looked up, fear settling in as she realized what she'd done. He opened his mouth, then closed it. She could feel rage emanating off him.

He finally set a smile on his face, clearly devoid of joy, and raised his foot from the puddle covering it. "Weak girl," he spat.

Poseidon pulled his jacket down and straightened his tie again. As he shoved past Henry, he stopped to declare, "You're fired." The squelch from his shoes echoed through the restaurant as he walked out. June sank to the ground and Henry fell next to her in time to slide his arm around her shoulders. They sat together for a few minutes until a server came and shooed them out.

Henry held June by the arm until they were outside, where she turned and fell into his chest. Tears started sliding down her face and he gripped her tightly.

"What am I supposed to do?" she whispered.

Henry didn't say anything for a moment, before he shrugged and the corner of his mouth tugged up. "We? I just got fired, you know."

June frowned at that and pulled back to look at him. Her eyes glistened in the dim light, and his face was riddled with concern. Overcome with emotion, she stood on her toes, bringing her face closer to Henry's. He leaned down, barely an inch away from her, and she stood as tall as she could to close the gap between them. His eyes widened as her lips touched his, and butterflies overtook her stomach. His eyes slid shut and he squeezed her tighter until she finally pulled back, breathing in sharply.

Blush had bloomed on her cheeks, and Henry looked at her awkwardly with a half grin. "That was nice."

June blinked, and they burst into laughter. He clasped her hand and began to walk toward her apartment, both of them still laughing.

"I'm sorry my life is so crazy. And I'm sorry you're wrapped up in this nonsense."

Henry pulled her to a stop and placed both hands on her face. "Hey, I wouldn't be here if I didn't want to be."

June nodded, and he brushed his lips against hers again before they continued walking.

"Thank you for coming out with me." Henry squeezed her hand, and she smiled in response.

"Thank you for asking. I had a nice time."

They both stopped in front of June's door and Henry let go of her hand. He ran a hand through his hair and looked around. "I guess—"

June cut him off. "Would you like to come up?"

"I'd like that. I'll have to go fetch my car later."

June looked around as if just realizing that they'd walked all the way home, and they laughed together again as she opened the door. This was the lightest she had felt in ages, despite the run-in with her enemy.

She led the way to the kitchen and stopped in her tracks in the doorway, narrowing her eyes at the dining table.

Henry stepped up behind her and asked, "What's wrong?"

"Asclepius," she muttered.

28

Henry looked around blankly while June glared at the table. "Can you see something?" he whispered, and June turned and looked at him, startled.

"Don't you see the snake there?"

He shook his head and looked again. A second later, he stumbled back. June eyed him curiously and he pointed, voice laced with fear. "That wasn't there a second ago. That's the snake that follows you!"

June turned back to face the snake and crossed her arms. "What do you want, Pius?"

The god writhed up from their scales, and Henry let out a high-pitched squeak, which June ignored. Seconds later, where a large black reptile had been, now sat Asclepius. They looked different than normal, with their gold makeup faded and normally slick hair mussed. June continued to stare, and the god finally broke the silence.

"That's a hell of a greeting for an old friend."

June scoffed. "Seriously? For the last time, we're not friends."

She turned to Henry and flourished her hand at them. "This is Asclepius, god of being a nuisance."

Asclepius looked ruffled at the insult but stuck his tongue in his cheek without saying anything. Henry stepped forward, raised his hand, then immediately dropped it and looked at June in bewilderment.

He stepped closer to the god and said, "I'm sorry, sir, I'm just not quite sure how to meet your . . . ah, type, yet." His voice trailed off and Asclepius laughed, hopping down from their seat on the edge of the table to stand.

They towered over Henry. "Well, first off, I'm not a sir. You can call me Asclepius, or—" they shot a dirty look at June "—Pius, as this one does. And second, traditionally anything from offerings of small animals to a bowing worship would be accepted. But I supposed we are in more modern times now, so a cup of tea will do."

Henry inclined his head awkwardly and moved to put the kettle on, busying himself by pulling mugs and silk tea pouches from the cabinet while Asclepius sat down. June slid into the chair opposite them and glared at them as they propped their elbows on the table and rested their chin on their hands.

"What do you want?" she asked, trying to keep the accusation from her voice. She was not happy with their last interaction and certainly wasn't going to let them off easily.

"Oh, nothing, just checking in to see what's happening."

June rolled her eyes. "Cut it, Pius. I'm tired of all you gods playing games with me. I'm not in the mood."

Asclepius sighed. "I'm serious, I'm just here to check in."

She eyed them suspiciously before saying, "I'm going to a gentleman's club."

Henry set a mug of tea in front of both of them. Pius picked it up, raised an eyebrow at June, and asked, "Oh?"

June nodded firmly. "Apparently Poseidon frequents the place, so I'll be going to try and find out where my mother is."

Asclepius laughed. "Brilliant! Because nothing could go wrong with a slight woman barely over five feet facing the god of the sea himself!"

June glared at them until they stopped laughing at their own comment. "I'll have you know that

I saw him today, actually, and came out in one piece."

Asclepius gave her an incredulous look. "And you're still looking for him? Didn't you turn him?"

June shook her head sadly. "I tried, but it didn't work . . . maybe I used it all up?"

Asclepius shrugged, then suddenly cocked their head, as if they'd heard someone yell their name. They began to morph down into a pile of scales, hissing, "Good luck," as they went.

Shock and confusion bled into her. "Pius?" she whispered. Then he was gone.

Henry finally walked back over from his spot by the sink and looked at the seat Asclepius had been sitting in, examining it as if the god might suddenly pop back up.

"Um, where did—" he hesitated " —they go?"

June shook her head. "I don't know."

Henry looked at the clock and moved to June, crouching in front of her. "I should go, but I'll come by tomorrow before you go to the club. Will you be okay?"

She nodded and gave him a peck on the cheek. "Thank you for tonight."

He smiled. "Of course."

Then June was alone. She looked around her empty apartment and sighed, placing a hand on her stomach. She looked down at it, but it was still flat and felt quite normal. "Are you in there?" she asked. Of course, nothing happened. She decided it was time for bed.

29

June woke suddenly as a bird whistled loudly outside her window. She sat bolt upright, a heavy wave of nausea washing over her, and threw back her blankets to run to the toilet. Her hands were clammy as she gripped the bowl, and she emptied her stomach of everything she'd eaten the night before. She looked down at her stomach, rolling her eyes at the thing that must be growing there, before wiping her mouth and standing to brush her teeth.

The world was strangely calm outside today. She fetched the paper from the door but saw no noticeable news on the front page, so she left it on the table for later.

As she busied herself making breakfast, a knock on the door sounded and Henry called out, "Good morning, sunshine!" before walking in. June smiled as he rushed over to kiss her on the cheek, standing behind her and wrapping his arms around her waist. She continued cutting fruit and he leaned down and murmured, "How did you sleep?"

June turned to face him and stood on her toes to kiss him. "Good, thank you. Breakfast?"

Henry shook his head. "No thanks, I'm just here for a few minutes. I'm supposed to head to the hospital today. They should have news about that odd sick spell."

June went pale and turned back to her work. She had forgotten about their rush to the hospital. "Oh? Did they say anything when we were there?"

Henry let go of her and shrugged, moving to sit at the table. "The doctor brought up pregnancy. He thought we were married. I said no and he said he was sure it must be something else then."

June dropped her knife on accident, and the loud clang made Henry whip his head up. She stepped back, gripping the counter and bracing herself against the edge while anxiety began to riddle her nerves.

Henry rose and asked, "Are you okay?"

June nodded, tears stinging her eyes, and tried to hide the reaction to hearing his words aloud. Of course she'd mentioned the possibility to Typhon and thought about it a bit because of that strange dream, but a doctor saying so made it so much worse.

In an instant, Henry was next to her. He pulled her into his arms gently and she began sobbing. "Hey, it's okay, we'll figure out what's wrong."

"Poseidon," June forced out through broken cries. "He—he attacked—" Her sobs renewed and a sudden look of understanding dawned on Henry's face.

"That's what you meant..." He trailed off and he squeezed her tighter.

Henry held her while she cried, humming a lulling tone. June sobbed and let everything out—things that she didn't realize she was holding onto. Her anger at her father. Hurt for her mother. Rage at Poseidon. Despair at this pregnancy. Everything flooded into her sobs, and soon she wasn't sobbing because of hurt anymore—tears were falling simply because they could.

It took a long while to recover, but once the tears had trickled off, Henry helped her to the table and dropped to a knee in front of her.

"Juniper Georgian, do not worry." His face was serious, and she sniffed, reaching up to wipe her nose with the back of her hand. "If you are, I will be here. If you'll have me. You have Ty too. And we will get your mother back."

June nodded, still sniffling as she began to tear up again. Henry shushed her and rose a bit to lean in and hug her. "It's okay. You're not alone in this."

She let out a rattled breath and squeezed him in thanks.

Henry stood and laughed lightly. "I suppose that if you're quite sure, there's no point for me to go to the hospital."

June thought of the strange man in her dream congratulating her, and she hiccupped. "I'm sure."

As if the universe needed her to prove the point, she stood suddenly and dashed to the bathroom for the second time that morning. Henry followed and rubbed her back as she threw up. He left for a minute and reappeared with a cool cloth that he placed on the back of her neck while she lay on the cold floor. He sat down next to her and kept rubbing her lower back until she felt she could move again.

"Why don't you go lie down? The club won't open until the afternoon, anyway." She nodded and he helped her stand, supporting her until they reached her bed. He looked around the room once she was tucked in and smiled at the paintings that decorated the walls. June watched his eyes and flushed. She hadn't looked at her own artwork in so long, and she felt embarrassed by his interest.

He left her after kissing her forehead and fluffing the pillow under her head, and June fell into a deep sleep.

June opened her eyes and looked around, surprised to see the bright marble room again. The same man she'd seen last time with the storm in his hair and eyes was sitting on the ground in front of her, legs crossed, with his eyes closed.

She crouched down and leaned forward. "Hello?"

His eyes snapped open and a broad smile spread on his face. "Hello, child. Back already?"

June nodded. "I suppose so. Do you know why I'm here?"

He chuckled pleasantly. "Your guess is as good as mine." He stood up and took June's hand.

She looked up at him, still confused over where she was and who he was, but she asked, "How did you know?"

The man held out his arm and they walked together while she held it. "I'm not sure what you mean."

June pointed at her stomach. "You know, this."

"Oh!" He laughed. "There's a great deal that I know. I can't exactly filter it out. I see one of you mortals and it's as if there's a radio station turned to your history."

She raised an eyebrow at the word *mortal*. "So, you're a god?"

He laughed again. "I guess you could say something like that."

She nodded. As they reached the grassy yard, she asked, "Do you know Poseidon? Asclepius?"

The man's face turned stormy, and June heard a loud boom in the distance. "Those two are terrible trouble. Avoid them at all costs."

June stopped and the man walked a few steps ahead before pausing. Her mind raced. "What about Typhon? What if I have to face Poseidon?"

The man looked at her curiously. "You trust who you feel deserves it. As for my brother . . .

if you must face him, kill him. He took down a terrible plague to the mortal world. And the other minors, such as that snake, have done nothing but help him. Poseidon needs to be stopped before he destroys Olympus and brings war to all realms."

June, body riddled with shock, opened her mouth to ask another question. Suddenly, the colors of the strange world faded, the loud boom from far away began, and the ground below her feet dropped out. She began to fall, this time too confused to scream, and began the same process as last time—falling through the stars to New York.

When June woke again, the sun was high in the sky. Although groggy, she didn't feel sick anymore, which she was thankful for. How was someone supposed to take down a powerful Olympian when they were sick nonstop from pregnancy? She shook her head and rubbed the crust from her eyes before venturing downstairs.

She was surprised to see Henry still there, comfortable on the couch with a book in hand. June smiled and he stood quickly.

"How are you feeling?"

She sat at the table and said, "Better."

Henry pulled a plate from the fridge and set it in front of June. "I thought you might be hungry, so I made a sandwich for when you woke up."

June's stomach grumbled on cue and she thanked Henry before digging in.

He sat across from her, watching intently. When she'd finished the last bite, he checked his watch and said, "It's nearly two. I think they should open soon. Do you still plan to go?"

June nodded. "Of course. I need to find my mother, and there's a chance she's there." She hesitated before continuing. "But, I think I need to be careful. I'm not ready to face Poseidon again, and I'm pretty sure I saw Zeus . . . who told me I had to kill him."

Henry blanched, and she explained her two strange dreams where she ventured to the marble room and spoke with the man with stormy eyes. Henry nodded along, and when she'd finished, he leaned back in his chair to ponder.

"Maybe we should get you a gun," he offered.

June laughed. "Me? No way. I could never handle one. Plus, what would a gun do against a god?"

Henry nodded again. "We'll figure something out then. Just try to avoid him. If you so much as glimpse the back of his head, run."

June agreed and rose, pausing to give Henry a kiss on the cheek before heading back upstairs to get ready.

Spades was a fifteen-minute walk from her house, and June took it quickly. Henry had argued with her, insisting that he should drive her or come with, but he finally listened to her pleas to go alone. She couldn't explain it, but as much as she liked Henry, they had really only known each other a short time, and he had worked for Don up until the day before. She didn't quite trust him yet.

So now she walked down the road, armed with nothing but the hope that her power would work in an emergency. Her mind was racing. What would she do if her mother was there? What if Poseidon was? What could she do if her power didn't work? She turned her face to the sky as she reached a corner and studied the dark gray clouds floating above.

"Hey, Zeus, if that was you, any help would be great," she whispered.

She received no response, but a small raindrop fell on her cheek. Then another, and another, until it was properly sprinkling. She yanked the collar of her coat up, grumbled about gods and storms, and wrapped her scarf around her head to protect her hair from the rain. The last thing she needed was for her hair to come out of its smoothing gel. She doubted a lion's mane would hold any power to stop any god. It would just get in the way.

She stepped up to the building that used to be Spades. The windows were boarded and the sign out front was decayed, so it read *SP DE*. She took a step closer to read a sign hanging on the door and was hit with a wave of dizziness. It felt different than what was normal lately, more like if someone had taken the powerful air around Athena and magnified it. She fought past the wave of sickness and stepped closer. The feeling intensified and she moved again. As soon as she was close enough to the door to press her nose against it, the sick feeling disappeared, and she looked up, confused. The sign was gone, and the paint was refreshed. It looked like a set of brand-new double doors. She turned and looked back at the street, which appeared the same.

She quickly backed up, and three steps took her through the odd heavy air that made her feel like falling over. From farther back on the street, the door looked as it did when she first approached. A wooden plank was nailed sideways over it, with a sign pinned up that she couldn't read. The paint was more than half chipped off, and she felt generally uninterested in going in.

She pushed herself back through again, stopping in front of the door. She laughed lightly as the dizziness faded and her mission came to the forefront of her mind. Whatever the strange wall was—because she was sure it was a wall and that it was magic—it must have been meant to deter humans away. She was definitely in the right place.

She tried the door and it swung open easily. As she stepped in, fifty pairs of eyes turned on her. She pushed her sunglasses up on her head and the men scattered about the club, hastily turning back to their games and conversations. She swung the door shut right as a familiar black car pulled up. She smiled before turning to look around the dimly lit room. She was shocked at what she saw. The window did not look boarded up from the inside. In fact, the street outside was crystal clear and bustling with people. It was as if the window wasn't there. Plush red carpet lined the floor and was covered in an array of rugs. The walls were made of richly colored oak, and sturdy wooden tables were scattered about, surrounded by men playing card games. A large bar sat near the back of the room, decorated with forgotten scotch glasses. The right side of the club held bookshelves, and the left a stage, with two beautiful women swaying to music and singing atop it.

June ignored the questions popping into her head, deciding to chalk it up to gods, and wove her way through the table maze toward the bar. She slid onto a stool and tapped the counter. "Gin Rickey, please."

The bartender's face flushed and his expression flickered between discomfort and confusion. "I'm sorry, ma'am, but we aren't allowed to serve women here."

June bolstered her confidence as much as possible and lowered her face to peer at him over her glasses. "Please don't make me repeat myself . . . or do something worse." Electricity crackled between them for a moment before she straightened up again.

The bartender bobbed his head and began working. "Right away then, Miss."

She turned on her stool while he poured gin and lime juice together, and she scanned the bar. She watched the women on stage for a moment, taking in the strange air around them. There were seats at the bottom of the stage full of more men, seemingly awestruck and sucked into their pull. June shook her head, trying to clear the fog that they caused. Some sort of sirens, it seemed. Their voices were haunting and beautiful. They wore silvery dresses and turned in time to the music together, the lights of the bar glinting off every sequin on their dress. She thought it was strange that women would sing in a gentleman's club if they couldn't be served here. As she looked closer, she noticed their dresses were actually thin enough to see through. She made out their undergarments and a blush rose to her cheeks, forcing her to look away. That made more sense.

When she blinked and looked up again, she noticed that many of the men at the tables were staring at her with malice in their eyes. As soon as she looked at each man, they turned back to their game in turn, but they seemed stiff, as if they were waiting for something.

Except for one. An older man sat near the bookshelves. June faltered as she recognized him as the god from her dreams. She was sure it was

Zeus. There seemed to be static in the air around him, and his amber suit reminded her of sunlight. She hadn't realized how muscular he was before and how much older he was than her. As the bartender slid a glass toward her, she leaned in to ask, "Who is that gentleman there?"

The bartender shook his head. "Not sure. He came in for the first time yesterday at open, and he didn't leave until close. Same thing again today. Apparently, he was sent by the heiress of something to wait."

June nodded. Eris kept her word, she thought. It was clear she had expected June to follow through. For what reason, she couldn't fathom. She carefully stood and walked toward him, trying to make herself appear larger than she was so the men peppered around the club wouldn't stare again.

She sat on the ottoman across from the stranger, setting her drink on a small accent table to his left. She decided that if Eris sent him, he should know what was going on.

"Hello, I believe you have something for me?" She smiled politely, and the man grinned and shook his head.

"No, ma'am, I can't say that I do."

A flicker of frustration passed over her face before she composed herself and leaned in so she was barely an inch away. "Look, I don't know if you know me, but I know you. And I know who sent you. I'm looking for a man named Don. Don Whittaker. You may know him as Poseidon."

The man in amber looked uneasy as he wriggled in his seat a bit. He looked around the room for a moment before jerking his head down in a nod you would only see if you were looking for it.

"This place isn't safe," he whispered. He reached into the drawer next to him and pulled out a scrap of paper and a pen.

He looked around again, and June understood he didn't want anyone to see. She braced her arms behind her body and spread them to block the view of him while he scribbled a note down.

He finished writing and shoved the paper into her hand, mumbling something about not enjoying being down with mortals. She smiled at him and stood, gingerly picking up her drink and striding back toward the bar. She slipped the paper into her pocket and left the untouched gin on the counter. When she turned and pulled her hand from her pocket, a large man grabbed her.

She was thrown to the ground and her arms were held out on either side of her while a third suit put a knee to her chest and knocked the breath out of her. She opened her mouth to scream, and a handkerchief was stuffed in. Her mind flashed back to the night in the alley, and all her rage and sadness and terror balled up in her chest. She began to thrash around and managed to knee the man on top of her between the legs. He rolled off with a groan, gripping his manhood and curling into a ball. She swung her leg wide around, skirt flying up, and kicked at the figure to her right. Her foot connected with his shin and he roared in pain, loosening his grip enough for her to yank her hand free and tear the sunglasses from her face. She rolled and stood, looking the last man holding her in the eye. He let go as panic lit up his face and he began to turn to stone.

June scrambled up as more men jumped from their seats and moved to join the fray. She managed to duck out of the way as one swung his meaty fist toward her. She heard it connect with bone as she wove through two tables. Confusion was making them dangerous, and a few pulled out switchblades or picked up glasses to throw. The women on stage began to sing louder, and June's heart raced in time to the music. Men lunged at her from every direction. It took all her focus to dodge and weave between them. One suit caught her by the shoulder and tore the thin fabric of her dress, and she turned and glared at him, stopping him in his tracks. He went gray, the bit of light-blue cotton still in his outstretched hand. June only watched for long enough to see one of his friends knock him down, causing his head to snap off and spin across the floor. She turned back to face the door and ran. The singers reached a crescendo in their song, and the harmony bore through June's brain, urging her to turn to them. She clapped her hands to her ears and tried to focus on the door ahead.

As she neared it, a small mousy-looking man that couldn't be much older than her stepped in front, blocking the way completely. She skidded to a stop and glared at him, but he looked up at the ceiling. A demented laugh erupted from his mouth, sounding like it belonged to a much larger body, and his face contorted. June stepped back, and a second later, his chest burst open. His pinstriped suit dropped to the floor in shreds, and she felt someone bump into her as she watched the man's skin turn in on itself. Terror set into her body as wings unfurled from his now bright-red feathered shoulder blades, and four bright orange eyes took place of his previous two blue ones, set around a massive black beak. The feathers stopped at his collarbone, giving way to taught red skin thinly covering a mass of muscle. June's eyes tracked to its feet and her stomach flipped at the large scaly talons now digging into the carpet.

She stood rooted in place as the monster threw its arms down and roared loud enough to shake the chandelier above her.

"June!" someone yelled from her side, and she was thrown sideways as the glass light fell, shattering on top of two suits that had lunged for her. The sound cracked around her, and small pieces of crystal and filament flew through the air. June crashed to the ground as terrifying howls and tearing sounds filled the room around her. She caught herself on her hands, wincing as she stood and saw blood blooming under embedded pieces of glass. She looked around and saw Henry a few feet away.

It took a moment to register that he was yelling "RUN!" over the din of singing, monstrous cries, and glass breaking. She bolted after him, turning to watch as more ten-foot-tall creatures climbed from their human skins around the room. Henry yanked her by the wrist and pulled her between tables and chairs, around the men still sitting in front of the siren-like singers in a daze. The pair turned to face the onslaught of monsters, and as they clambered over each other to reach them, June yelled, "We have to go!"

She took a step forward before turning to Henry and realizing he was staring up at the women. She reached out and yanked on his arm, but he didn't budge. A furtive glance behind them warned her that she had only moments to run before the monsters would reach them.

She quickly reached over her shoulder and yanked a bit of her sleeve off that was already torn, shredding it into two small scraps in desperation. She reached up and shoved a piece into each of Henry's ears before grabbing his hand and bolting between two suits stuck in their trance. Thankfully, he followed her this time.

As they ran around the right side of the bar, the terrifying creatures lunged after them. Henry jumped over an overturned chair, landed in front of the door easily, and threw it open. June pushed through the wall of magic and out to the sidewalk behind him, where he stopped and bent over, resting his hands on his knees while panting. June watched as the flying red things pounded into the wall, toppling over each other. She glared at each one of them, and the three at the front turned to stone in front of her. She fell to the ground then, exhausted. Henry was behind her as she sat, bracing his hands under her arms.

"Come on, June, we have to move." As he said it, she saw the magic waver, glimpsing a bit of the polished door before it returned to a clear image of an abandoned building. She half stood, watching as a man in a suit pushed past the creatures and through the wall. The moment his foot touched the sidewalk, Henry and June ran again. They moved as fast as possible, both gasping for air. They took sharp corners and weaved around pedestrians that threw them dirty looks before they finally slowed to a trot near June's apartment. Henry stopped and looked around, and June placed her hands on her hips, wincing and breathing heavily. How they got out of there alive, she had no idea.

Henry finally caught his breath and asked, "What was all that?"

June grabbed the stitch in her side and screwed up her face. "Don's protection, I think."

He nodded and motioned to the front door, and they walked in together. June stopped halfway up the stairs. Turning to Henry, she frowned. "What were you doing there?"

He had a sheepish look on his face and shrugged. "I thought you might need help. I was worried."

June nodded and finished the climb to the kitchen. Henry slumped into a chair and she slid down the wall to the floor. A long beat passed before Henry scrubbed his face and sighed.

"So, what happened? Was he there?"

June shook her head and remembered the paper in her pocket. "No, but I think I may have met Zeus."

His jaw dropped and she stood, pulling the scrap out and tossing it on the table. Henry grabbed it quickly and unfurled it. "Trust no one. Times Square at noon." They looked at each other, confused.

30

Typhon drifted over a large gate, spikes breaking his breeze as he jumped the fence. He shook his head as he looked at the massive manor in front of him. It looked almost like a warehouse from the outside—a massive iron box with black windows. As he rounded the front, the door swung wide open. He took himself down and landed on the front step, straightening his jacket as he stepped in. A small, balding man stood with his hand on the lever, bowing slightly.

"Good evening, Last Titan. Mistress Eris is in the lounge."

Typhon nodded firmly and headed to the right, but the old man cleared his throat. Typhon turned to see him pointing to a nearly closed door in the opposite direction, and his lip twitched as Typhon walked that way.

He approached the door and froze in his tracks before he made it through the frame.

Eris was in the room, indeed. She was perched on the back of a couch facing a large fireplace. With a black silk robe falling from her shoulder and barely covering her waist, Typhon could clearly see the outline of her breasts against the firelight. He took a step back as she threw her head back and moaned loudly.

As Typhon was about to turn, he caught sight of a head bobbing between her legs, her feet resting on the poor bastard's shoulders. He shook his head and summoned a breeze to shoot through the house.

As he explored and tried to shake the image of what he'd walked in on, he realized that *house* was an understatement. In his personally guided tour, he found sixteen bedrooms, nine bathrooms, a piano room, and a restaurant-sized kitchen — not to mention the entire lower level of staff accommodations.

He finally stopped in the foyer again, nearly tripping over one of his leaves while he tried not to bang into a massive sculpture. He straightened and pulled his jacket down, and when he looked up, Eris was standing in front of him with her arms crossed and a grim look on her face. At least she had tied her robe up.

"Spying, are we?" She raised an eyebrow at him.

"Just killing time while you finished molesting some poor mortal."

Eris laughed, and the sharp sound echoed around them. "It's not molesting if they come asking."

Her eyes twinkled as she turned back to the lounge and motioned for Typhon to follow. He felt a bit green as he thought about that. If any of the gods were to be given the title *of the whores*, it should be Eris.

They settled into couches opposite each other, and Eris crossed her legs and clasped her hands on top of her knee before leaning forward, an expectant look on her face.

Typhon cleared his throat, trying not to think of what had been done on these couches. "I've come to seek an alliance."

Eris cocked her head, frowning for a moment before bursting into laughter. Typhon's jaw twitched and her laugh faded as she regarded his tense expression. Her eyes widened. "You can't be serious?"

He motioned around. "You've been here for a hundred years. Don't you think it's time to actually help somewhere?"

Eris jumped up, and her robe fell open from the motion. Typhon flinched as she yelled, "I do help! I help Poseidon every *fucking* day."

Typhon sighed and motioned for her to sit back down, which she did with a huff.

"I know you've been on his side in the past, but you can't possibly believe in him anymore. He's the reason for June's situation, and in turn, responsible for the demise of someone you were close with, correct?"

Blush rose into her cheeks as she swore, then waved her hand. "That was just a minor casualty. No one important."

Typhon smirked. "Oh, you just lured an innocent to the park for a quickie that was interrupted then?"

"Exactly. It's not my problem if she mistook role-playing for something else."

Typhon leaned back and crossed his arms. "You're really happy being on his side then?"

Eris' face fell as she picked a nail, eyes trained down. "I don't have a choice."

"What do you mean? Look around! You've managed a building plant for years, swept hundreds of men off their feet, and managed to secure this mansion. You've become just as important as him here."

She looked up sadly. "I'm just a prisoner in this war, Ty. Head of recruitment because he forces me to be, and living in a pretty cage."

Understanding dawned on him then. "This isn't your place, is it?"

She shook her head.

"Fight back then!"

She met his gaze and her throat bobbed. "I've tried." She stood slowly, holding eye contact with Typhon before whispering, "It's not easy to leave." Then, with a loud cracking sound, she blinked out of existence.

He leaned forward and pinched the bridge of his nose. This was going to be a lot harder than he thought.

31

"Maybe it means we *shouldn't* go there," Henry offered, voice high with anxiety.

June shook her head. "It has to mean that I'm supposed to. I'm just not sure what day, or where, exactly. That's a massive spread of buildings."

Henry shrugged and picked at another piece of glass in her hand. She winced and glanced at the clock on the wall.

"Maybe I should go now? If he's meant to be there at noon on some day, I could look for any hiding places or anything out of the ordinary ahead of time."

Henry looked at her and opened his mouth as if he was going to protest, but her face was set with determination. He instead said, "Okay, let's go."

June cocked her head and looked at him, confused.

"I know that you're anxious to get your mom back and figure out this debt. I would be too, if my parents were around and it were them. So we'll go."

June sighed. "I can go on my own. I doubt it'll be dangerous."

Henry rolled his eyes and reached out, pulling her to his lap. He grabbed her face in his hands and looked her in the eye, smiling at the fact her glasses were gone. "Juniper Georgian, when are you going to accept that I am here to help?"

"I know you keep saying that, but you were just questioning me on *his* behalf not long ago."

He dropped his hands to her waist. "Yes, June, but a lot has changed since then, right? I don't work for him anymore, he's hurt you, he's taken your mother, and apparently there are fucking gods interfering among us that are worse than him!"

June broke into a grin and laughed. "Okay then. We can get dinner afterward?"

"Done."

He held her waist as she stood, and they walked downstairs hand in hand. June grabbed a coat to cover her torn dress with. Henry insisted that they take his car, even though it was less than a ten-minute walk, and a matter of minutes later, they were parked on the corner of forty-second street.

June looked around anxiously, worried that there were more suits outside. Finally, she sighed and stepped out of the car. Nothing jumped out at her, and she joined Henry on his side, taking his hand and walking down the road.

They ventured together in silence, both looking around. Many of the buildings here were empty, aside from the hotel to their left. They walked a bit further and came upon a construction lot. Tall steel beams stuck up in the sky, surrounded by a half-built brick wall. June pointed and Henry nodded. She couldn't tell if it was in the process of being built or had crumbled over time. The bricks looked old and were covered in grime. The parking lot was muddy and peppered with potholes, and vines climbed the beams. They crossed the road, and when they stopped in front of the building, June was hit with mild dizziness. She stepped closer, and the feeling became stronger. She quickly moved back, pulling Henry with her.

He stumbled and stopped next to her. "The air is so . . . heavy," he murmured, looking anxiously at the wall between them and the dilapidated structure.

June nodded. "It's just like Spades."

Henry's eyes went unfocused, and he stared into the distance for a moment before snapping his fingers. He spun to face June and exclaimed, "I know why this is familiar! Don — or Poseidon — used to have an office at the department. When he visited, if you walked near the door, you suddenly forgot why you were there. There was an emergency once where someone broke out of their cell, and I had to focus to get through the weird invisible wall, after I turned from it a few times." He looked a bit embarrassed. "When I did finally get through, I threw up in a trash can before I could tell him and my captain what happened."

June shook her head. "This one almost feels stronger, though, like there's a bunch of different types of magic feeding into it."

"Maybe there is." Henry took her hand and led her back toward the car. "We'll figure it out."

They drove in silence while June tried to think of what to do. If Poseidon was there, how was she supposed to get in? And how was she supposed to settle this debt when he seemed hell-bent on wreaking havoc on her life? Maybe the only answer was to kill him. But if her power didn't work against him, what would she do?

"You know, I think I've handled this all fairly well so far," Henry said, "but I've got to be honest. My mind hasn't stopped spinning since I met Typhon."

June's head snapped up and she looked at him. "What do you mean?"

"I mean, I never once thought about the possibility that the gods were real. To me, they were all myth. It all was. I swallowed all this new information down because I care about you, but the further we go into this, the more I wonder if I've gone crazy and this is all my imagination. Maybe I'm actually strapped to a table somewhere having my head electrocuted." His tone was joking, but June's brow furrowed with concern.

"You don't have to do this . . ."

Henry reached out and squeezed her hand. "I do. I want to be here for you. This has been a lot to process."

June didn't get a chance to respond as Henry stopped the car. He went around to her side to help her out, and she continued to ponder as they walked down the road together. Someone bumped into her, and her heart rate spiked. Still jumpy and afraid from their experience earlier, she raised her head quickly, relieved to see it was a normal man. She opened her mouth to apologize for not watching where she was going, but before she could say a word, he was marble. Henry froze in place as well and stared. June swore.

She looked around quickly, making sure no one was watching, and quickly removed her coat and threw it over the now frozen form.

Henry's voice was thick as he whispered, "So, that's how it works."

She looked at him with pain in her eyes. "Can you please help?"

He held up his hands and grinned. "Are you going to kill me too?"

June began to tear up and Henry lowered his arms, his eyes softening. "Hey, I'm sorry, I was just—"

June cut him off and yelled, "Just stop!"

Henry looked lost for a moment, and he opened his mouth to speak before closing it again. He looked around, and June watched as his face dropped.

"I can't do this," he whispered, before stepping back. He turned and walked away quickly, breaking into a jog down the road. She watched as he picked up speed and disappeared at the end of the block.

June leaned against the building next to her and put her head in her hands. Why couldn't this stupid power cooperate? She screamed up at the sky loudly before shaking her head, trying to force the replay of what happened from her mind.

It took her nearly an hour to recover. She rose from where she'd sank to the ground and brushed off her skirts. Looking around, she made sure that no one was watching before she began to drag the statue to the gallery. She hadn't planned to turn any more men, at least not on purpose. She felt terrible. What if this one had a family, a wife? She dragged him inch by inch. The normal five-minute walk turned into over a half hour, and her muscles screamed in protest the entire way. Drenched in sweat, she dragged the man into the diner and set him next to William, who she looked at sadly. She touched her father's hand and whispered, "I wish you were still here, so you could help."

Feelings of hopelessness and overwhelm began to weigh her down, and unsure of what to do with herself next, she went to bed.

32

June opened her eyes to find herself in the familiar glistening white marble room, but something was wrong this time.

She looked around, watching as the top parts of the marble columns crumbled. The massive opening in the ceiling that let in the sun was falling in on itself. The sky itself was no longer bright, but gray and dreary. Lightning arced through the sky, and she turned her head up to look. She dove out of the way as a chunk of gold ceiling the size of a car fell where she had just been standing. The sounds around her finally came into focus, and she heard people screaming in an odd language. She grabbed the side of her head to try to stop the ringing in her ears. Her vision was blurred, but she could make out other people in white robes, running this way and that.

She scrambled up quickly, shaking the daze from her head, just as a piece of marble to her right crashed down, shaking the floor and causing a loud cracking sound to echo through the air. June swiveled around and watched as two figures ran through the exit she had visited before, and she took off after them, dodging and weaving as pieces of rock and gold tumbled down around her. Screams filled her ears as she pumped her arms and ran. She dove through the arch as it fell in on itself.

Landing hard on the ground on her stomach, she groaned and pushed herself up, suddenly aware of the fact that the screams had stopped and the world was quiet. She stood and brushed the dirt from her dress. Where was the robe she normally wore in this dream? She looked up to see over twenty people staring at her in mute silence. Some threw their hands up and gasped, and some glared at her with open hatred. She lifted her hand and quietly said, "Hello."

"June?" The voice called her name from somewhere in the crowd. "June!" it exclaimed frantically, and she watched as Typhon pushed forward through the mass of people, splitting the group in two. He ran to her and embraced her, but she was too shocked to move.

"Ty? Why are you here?"

He pulled back, and she got a good look at him. He was Typhon, but also not. His skin had a red glow to it, and he'd sprouted horns. His deep voice was the same, but he was taller than normal and much more muscular as well, and he was wearing a piece of the white cloth that made up most robes, but it was only tied around his waist. June looked away and blushed. "Can you maybe put a shirt on?"

Typhon looked down and said, "Oh!" before waving his hand in front of him in a swirl. Suddenly, he stood in front of June in the same way he'd appeared through her childhood—nicely pressed suit, driver's cap, normal human-looking skin, no horns.

June smiled and gave him a proper hug. "What's going on here?"

He shook his head. "It's quite the story. What are *you* doing here?"

She shrugged. "I've become a frequent visitor. This is my dream, after all." Typhon froze and looked at her curiously, before glancing behind him and taking her hand to lead her away from the crowd.

The sky was still dreary, but the sounds of crashing and stone had stopped, and she couldn't hear screams anymore as they walked together in the grass. Typhon stopped them among some wildflowers and sat down, and June followed suit.

Typhon sighed. "June, this isn't a dream. This is Olympus. Who knows how you found it, but you're not meant to be here."

June's jaw dropped as she looked around. It made sense. This place was gorgeous, unearthly, and felt something akin to heavenly. "I can't help when I come. I fall asleep in bed and wake up here. Then here crumbles and I wake up back in bed."

Typhon held up his hands. "Hold on, what do you mean it crumbles?"

June explained her last two visits, her meeting with the gray-eyed man, and how the ground would fall out from under her and she would fall through stars.

Typhons face went white. "June, I don't think you were dreaming the last couple times. I think you were seeing prophecy."

June blinked at him, confused.

"It's rare, but sometimes mortals, when exposed to a god at one time or another, develop some sort of power based on their personality. Normally it's small, something like their memory improving or they are a bit stronger than before. It's possible that since you spent your entire childhood with me, and then were blessed by another god, that something more came out."

June threw up her hands. "Why does this keep happening to me!"

Typhon furrowed his brow. "I think there's someone you need to meet."

June stood and followed as he led her further through the grass. A tall marble wall, maybe to whatever was behind the large room she had appeared in, ran parallel to their right, and a dense forest sat to their left. Wildflowers speckled the grass beneath their feet, and June swore she heard something, or someone, whisper from a tree as she passed close to it. They walked for a few minutes, until Typhon stopped. June, who'd been so focused on the grass and flowers at her feet, nearly ran into him. She stepped back and looked up, sucking in a sharp breath.

A large stable, unlike anything she'd ever seen, stood in front of them. It had gilded walls, with deep mahogany support beams. There were six separate stalls, and a horse twice her height stood in each one. They were bright white, with a golden sheen to them, deep black eyes, and gold-tipped manes. June stepped forward to look closer, and one of the mares snorted. The sound was like a cannon boom, and she guessed, based on its size, that it likely sounded the same when it began running.

She stepped back next to Typhon who leaned down and whispered, "Apollo's steeds." June nodded, and Typhon cupped his hands around his mouth to yell, "Hey, Apollo!"

A golden head popped up in the second-to-last stall, and June giggled nervously at the start it gave her. The man's hair looked like hand-spun gold, as if something had created thread from sunlight and carefully sewn every strand of hair into his head. His skin was beautifully tanned, and he had what June could only describe as perfect features. He seemed to grow slightly smaller as he approached them, shrinking to Typhon's height as he stopped in front of June and held out his hand, an impish grin on his face.

"Hi," he said, winking.

June blushed and looked down, only to realize that Apollo was completely naked aside from a pair of small shorts. She looked away as Typhon smacked Apollo's outstretched hand. "Be decent. We need your help."

June caught a flicker of irritation pass over Apollo's face before he spun in a quick circle, rich purple robes appearing as he slowed to a stop.

Even in dark clothing, the god radiated light. His skin glowed and his teeth sparkled when he grinned. "What can I do for you?" He addressed

Typhon but kept eye contact with June. She was sure that her face was still red.

Typhon cleared his throat and motioned away from the stable. "Perhaps where there aren't ears?"

Apollo agreed and led the way to a small bench where he sat. Typhon and June found a place on the ground, and Apollo's grin widened, as if he was proud of himself for sitting higher than the others.

"This is June, my ward. And I believe she may have an ability that will interest you."

Apollo waved his hand nonchalantly. "Yes, I know all about our new little mortal protector. Likes to cause trouble and kill off men to protect the women, yeah?" He winked at June and her embarrassment colored her cheeks.

"Yes, well, I believe we also may have a new oracle in the making."

Apollo took on a puzzled look and leaned in toward June, eyeing her up and down. "No. Not possible."

Ty blanched. "What do you mean?"

"All my oracles are already in place, and I have an innate connection to all of them." He wagged his finger at June's stomach. "That one, however, may be a different story. I do sense the power there."

June self-consciously placed a hand over her belly and looked down. It had been well over a month since the attack from Poseidon, but it was still too early to feel anything. "So, even though I'm not an oracle, this baby could be giving me visions."

Apollo jerked his chin down in a nod. "It's not unheard of. Although, it is strange, if you are carrying a human child. You are just mortal, correct?"

Typhon picked at a cuticle, looking uneasy. "I assume so, but we're not sure. Haven't really had a chance to test it."

Apollo nodded again and clapped his hands before standing. "Well, this has been nice, but I really must be going."

Typhon scrambled to his feet. "Wait! There was a vision. That's why we came."

Apollo lowered himself back to his seat, intrigue clear on his face. "Go on."

June launched into the story of her dream of everything going dark and falling through the ground. Apollo's face paled, his glow dimming for a moment before asking, "And you're sure of this?"

June confirmed, and the god placed his chin in his hand, looking lost in thought.

"Do you know what caused the fall in the main hall today?"

June shook her head. Apollo's face looked grim. "Poseidon has been wreaking havoc on the mortal world of late. Then he brought it here. I believe he has the intention of taking down Olympus, or someone does. Either way, the monsters he stole from Hades were sent here, and there was a bit of a battle before you showed."

"But why? Why go through all this trouble?"

Apollo shrugged. "Boredom perhaps. Or it's just that he really wants Zeus' position. Crazies crave power, and he's been slighted for too long."

June nodded. "What do we do then?"

Typhon whispered, "Kill him."

June turned her head quickly and looked at her friend. How did one kill a god?

As if he'd read her mind, Apollo said, "He can only be killed here. If he dies down there, then he'll just come back here. But if someone can force him to come here in his mortal form, and Zeus can neutralize him, then we won't have to worry about it anymore."

June nodded and looked around thoughtfully. "How?"

Apollo shrugged. "If you're able to hop back and forth, maybe you can bring someone with you."

"I only come here in my sleep!"

Apollo laughed. "You'll have to figure it out." He promptly rose, spun, and disappeared in a flash of light.

Typhon sighed and stood as well, reaching down to help June up. He gave her a quick squeeze and said, "We'll figure it out. I have to help clean up here, but see if you can use Henry as a test to get him up here. I'll be down soon." June nodded into his chest and closed her eyes.

June opened her eyes in the dark, blinking to try and see. Normally those dreams lasted until early morning, but she felt like she was in bed now. This bed felt different, though. It was hard, and her blanket was gone. She heard a sound a few feet away, and her head swiveled of its own accord. A slit of light appeared, casting a dim glow on the room.

It was not her own room. It was small and the walls were unfinished, with rough concrete slapped here and there. The floor was bare. She looked down at her bed and was shocked to see that it was just a thin mattress on the floor. The door opened wider and her mouth and body moved on their own again.

She sat up in the bed and with a hoarse voice asked, "Are you going to let me go now?"

June's breath caught. It wasn't her own voice that cracked across the room, it was her mother's. The person on the other side of the door stepped in, and June was shocked. She tried to gasp and throw her hand to her mouth, but her body wouldn't move. Asclepius stood there, holding a plate with dry food on it.

Asclepius appeared more beaten down than before. The last of their golden glow was gone, and their shoulders were slumped. Bruises took up half their face, and when they shuffled into the room, they seemed to have a limp. Asclepius set the plate down at the end of the bed and began to slowly shuffle out. As they reached the door, they stopped for a minute, as if they thought of offering some kind words.

"Let me go home!"

Helen's voice made Asclepius flinch, and they turned and looked at her sadly. "I'm sorry. I have orders."

Suddenly, June was flung from her mother's body.

June slammed back into her own body, gasping for air. She sat up and looked down at her stomach, shaking. Her fingers trembled as she laid her hand there.

She breathed heavily. "What was that?"

Of course, there was no response. She placed her head in her hands as she tried to catch her breath. The sun rose slowly outside, and as it peeked over the horizon and birds began to sing, she calmed herself.

She forced her body out of bed, still feeling disoriented by the dreams—although, they really couldn't be dreams, could they? If Apollo and Typhon were right, she was visiting Olympus. And she'd just seen her mother. Or been her mother. But if the baby was giving her some power of oracle, that would have been a vision of the future. She just had no way of knowing when exactly.

Her mind raced as she went through the motions of making her morning cup of tea. She so missed having coffee, but knowing the baby would make her throw it up, she begrudgingly drank the green tea, just to have something warm. She was too lost in thought to even notice the mild nausea that rose up, and her first sip pushed it back down. She leaned against the counter, sipping slowly and pondering the events of the night. She felt exhausted, like she hadn't actually slept.

She finally snapped her head up and looked at the clock. It was eleven in the morning. Henry should be here by now to go to Time's Square. The memory of yelling at him to leave slammed into the front of her mind, and her heart hurt. She hoped that he knew she hadn't meant it. He was normally so persistent. Would he really leave for good? She finished her tea and set the glass in the sink. She would have to go alone.

As she began to dress, opting for a plain dress and flat shoes, a tap sounded on her window. She looked up and saw Asclepius there, and anger washed over her. She balled her fists and swore at the snake, but they tapped again. They didn't stop tapping until she moved to unlock and swing open the window.

"What do you want?" she hissed as they slithered in and materialized on her bed.

"I don't have much time."

June looked them up and down, realizing they looked similar to her vision. The gold makeup was mostly gone, with only a bit of shimmer on their cheekbones, and bruises were blooming on their neck and other cheek. It was soon, then.

"Leave. I know you're working with Poseidon." As those words left her, something clicked. Pius had known when she was going to the factory, then suits had shown up. They'd known when she went out with Henry, then Poseidon had shown. They had been reporting back all along. She reached forward and grabbed their arm, dragging them to the window.

"No!" they exclaimed. "I've made a mistake! He took Henry too. I don't want to help him anymore. His vision has changed so much from when we started."

June paused. "He . . . took Henry?" Rage bubbled up like lava in her chest as Pius looked at her helplessly. "What do you mean *took*?"

Asclepius sighed and folded their hands. "Suits were waiting nearby when you yelled. They threw a bag over his head and took him."

June's heart felt like it broke in two. Henry — her Henry — was gone? Just like her mother! Her rage dropped and swirled in her stomach. She thought she would be sick. What was she to do now? Even if he didn't want to be involved, she couldn't let Poseidon get away with this. And

Henry had been her first kiss. She . . . cared about him.

Asclepius continued to look at her with that strange mix of helplessness and pity. She snapped. She picked up the heavy silver hairbrush from her table and threw it at them.

"Get out!" she screamed.

It clunked against their face and fell to the ground. They threw their hand up to cover the eye that the broadside of the brush had hit and looked at her sadly one last time before dropping into a pile of scales and disappearing.

June threw herself on the bed and began sobbing. How could she let this happen? Now she had to figure out how to get both her mother and Henry back. She was meant to go to that building at noon. Noon!

She jumped up, quickly wiping her tears, and checked the clock. It was ten past now. She swore and righted her dress before running downstairs. She'd bet that both people she loved were being held there if that was Poseidon's hideout.

She rushed through the door and ran, nearly knocking over an old woman on the sidewalk. It took her a few minutes to reach forty-second street. She skidded to a stop in front of the building's magical wall. Now, she couldn't feel the electric humming of it like the day before. She held out her hand and waved it in the air where the wall should be, but she found nothing. She suddenly felt as if someone was watching her, and arm still outstretched, leaning forward, she looked to her right. A woman was standing with a child, watching her. She realized she must have looked crazy. The woman had a strange look on her face and the child was laughing. June blushed and put her arm down, smiling at the pair.

"Just checking. I thought there was a vent blowing upward here."

The woman quickly ushered her son away, casting a sidelong glance at June before she went. June sighed and turned back to the building. She swallowed hard and took a step forward. Then another. Nothing happened. No terrible wave of sickness came over her. She kept walking, careful to avoid the muddy puddles and piles of discarded car parts that took up most of the empty lot in front of the building. The building itself cast a shadow over her, and she shivered. She kept moving and approached the door of the half-completed building. She pressed her ear to the heavy iron. Not hearing anything on the other side, she swung it open with a loud creaking sound. No one was on the other side.

Two staircases stood on either side of the main room, and the whole area seemed to be larger than her apartment. Another heavy door stood opposite her. The floor was half concrete, half wood peppered with dents and burn marks. Sconces hung on the walls, some nearly falling off, and she noticed that the staircases were falling apart as well. She approached the one on the left and was shocked to see that nearly every other step was missing, and burn marks decorated the wall that held a railing. She wasn't sure if there had been a fire here or if a fire-breathing creature had come through. She wouldn't be surprised by the latter anymore.

As she lifted her foot to climb a step, she spotted a door near the back of the room and went that way instead. She listened at it once again, and upon hearing nothing, she pushed it open.

Her jaw dropped as she stepped into the small room. The walls looked like obsidian. Purple light danced around her as candles placed in each corner reflected off the dark glassy surfaces. In the center of the room, just three feet in front of her, stood a round table. It came up to her waist and held a small silver bowl on it. She stepped forward and looked in.

The bowl appeared to hold water. As she lowered her face to look closer, the liquid rippled. She squinted and began to see images form. Shapes warped and swam until she could see a clear picture of Henry standing with Poseidon. They looked as if they were having a lively conversation. Henry mimed shooting a gun, and Poseidon roared with laughter. What was this? The image shifted, and it was her mother, lying in bed with Asclepius. The water form of Helen snuggled in to the god's chest, and they seemed to wink up at June. She wrinkled her nose, mildly grossed out, and the image warped again. This time, she had to squint and look closer. As she moved, the image in the bowl did too. She realized that it was her, from the back. She watched as someone stepped forward, holding a gun, and pointed it at her back. The hand in the image cocked the revolver, and she heard a click behind her. She slowly lifted herself up.

"Well, well, June. What do we have here?" Eris' sickeningly sweet voice filled the room.

June turned slowly and grimaced. Eris was standing in the doorway, pistol in hand, legs shoulder-width apart, pointing the barrel at June's face. Eris flicked the tip of the gun toward the bowl and June flinched.

"What's going on there?"

June glanced down and back up again. The image still showed the gun being pointed at her. "I'm honestly not sure. I'd say the water is showing me the future, but maybe not." She stepped back an inch. Eris kept the weapon trained on her. "What are you doing here, Eris?"

The goddess stepped closer. "Why don't you tell me that? Why are you lurking in an abandoned building?"

June tried to step back again, and Eris shook her head. "If you must know, I'm looking for my mother—and Henry. Don took them."

Eris lowered her gun. "I thought you were working with him for a moment. I'm looking for a way out of his captivity."

June breathed a sigh of relief and asked, "What do you mean?"

Eris shook her head as she tucked the firearm into the back of her skirt. "Doesn't matter. How were you able to see anything in that?"

She motioned at the bowl of water and June shrugged. "Can't you?"

Eris shook her head and stepped up to the bowl, bracing both hands on either side and glaring into the surface. "Only Poseidon or his descendants can. Even though Apollo is the god of prophecy, ol' Donny boy wanted a bit of it for himself. He had this crafted so he could glimpse the future. I've been told it's only partially useful. Sometimes it shows the past, but otherwise it's like having your own little oracle." She stroked the rim of the bowl and a cold feeling dropped into June's stomach. The mention of an oracle again made her feel sick. If she had any doubts about the father of her child, they would have been gone with this interaction. Not only was the child in her Poseidon's, which would likely give her the same abilities, but Typhon was also sure it was a new oracle. She sighed and then froze as a banging sound from outside the room sounded.

Eris motioned at June and hissed, "Hide!"

June obeyed, ducking under the tablecloth and holding her breath. She could see Eris' shadow through the thin fabric, and she hoped no one could see her.

Eris took her weapon out once again and left the room. Dead silence rang in June's ears as she waited. Suddenly she heard Eris exhale loudly. "You scared me, Don! I was just doing a search—" Her voice was cut off and she emitted a choking sound.

"You're a snake. Even more so than Asclepius. I know you helped that little brat out and you're trying to leave me for Typhon. You really had the nerve to turn up here after being gone for days?"

Eris choked again and June threw her hand up over her mouth, tears prickling at the corner of her eyes. Poseidon threw Eris down, and June watched as her shadow fell to the ground in the middle of the large room. She could see the hulking outline of Poseidon step over the woman, and June bit her hand to keep quiet.

"You've fulfilled your use. Take a message up to Zeus for me. I'm done playing games. He will step down, or I will kill every one of his agents. I've found a way around his walls. It won't be just here, but in the void."

Eris whimpered. A flash of light made June wince and the loud bang of a gunshot echoed around. Don held his position with his weapon still pointed at Eris for a moment, before stepping back. June couldn't see anything but the outline of Eris' body for five long, quiet breaths.

Suddenly, Poseidon's outline appeared in the doorframe. June flinched and squeezed her hand tighter around her own mouth. The god ambled in and placed his hands on top of the table, causing it to shake.

"Little pond, show me the future." His voice sounded strangely affectionate, as if he cared for the porcelain dish, and all the traces of its normal roughness were gone.

June held her breath as Poseidon stood mere inches from her. He began laughing, and she shook as cold terror seeped into her bones.

"Yes, that's right. She will be caught. Show me when she will come here." The water splashed a bit, and his laugh faded. "That's not right."

June watched as he stepped back and turned, peeking out through the door, before turning back to the bowl. "Stupid thing. Get it together." He slammed his hand down next to it, making the table shake and the water splash. He turned, grumbling, and began to close the door behind him. June caught a few of his words before the door closed with a click. "Here, now? Ridiculous. And Henry? No, way."

She stayed frozen in place and listened to his heavy footsteps fade. She waited for the count of sixty before climbing out from her hiding place and glancing at the bowl. The image of Henry running from suits was spinning in the bowl. He ran into the building she stood in, yanked open the door, and gave her a hug. Then the image reset. June shook her head and turned to the door.

She breathed deeply for another minute, before reaching out to turn the handle. It stopped halfway in its arc and wouldn't move anymore. She pushed on the door. It didn't budge. Her heart raced as she pushed and turned and tried to get it to move. Her tears returned and she turned her back to the door, sliding down to the floor. She was scared to make too much noise, but it was clear that Poseidon had locked her in.

33

Hours passed. June knew it by the way her stomach grumbled and her bladder swelled against her undergarments. She desperately needed a bathroom, a hot meal, and a cup of coffee to combat the swimming in her head.

Since the room had no windows, she had no other way to track the time aside from the alarm bells her body set off. Even the candles gave her no indication, somehow still burning at the same level as when she walked in. She sighed and stood. Maybe she should scream for help? But what if the wrong type came? No, best to stay quiet. If the bowl was to be trusted, Henry would be coming. How he was to get away from Poseidon, she didn't know. She walked to the silver bowl and peered down. The same image was still looping around.

"When is it going to happen?" she asked aloud.

The water stopped and began to move the image backward. June rolled her eyes. Maybe Poseidon was right and it was on the fritz. A wave of nausea rose in her chest and she placed a hand on her stomach. A thought struck her. She leaned down close and whispered into the bowl.

"Show me our future."

The water stopped again before it began to swirl. It moved faster and faster, splashing up the sides of its container as it went. June became dizzy from watching and blinked, trying to right herself. Her eyes crossed, and she suddenly fell sideways, the world going black as she hit the floor.

When she opened her eyes, she was in a hospital bed. Sweat drenched her brow, and a doctor swam into focus next to her.

"Breathe, breathe, and push!" he exclaimed.

June's body seized, and her stomach clenched as she pushed down. She suddenly realized where she was — in labor. She looked to the side and didn't see Henry. Her heart sank. The doctor made her push twice more while a nurse held her hand, and she gasped between contractions. Her mind was telling her she was in pain, but if she focused, she could tell that she actually couldn't feel anything.

It was a strange experience. She pushed again, and the doctor yelled, "Congratulations!"

The room around her was still out of focus, and she blinked to try and clear the fuzziness. She watched as the doctor raised something up into the air and smacked it. The thing glowed like a small sun, almost too bright to look at. It hit her then. Her child. A piercing scream erupted from it as the doctor began to lower it into a blanket held by a nurse. The babe screamed louder, and the doctor's hands released it, turning to stone inches from the bundle. The gray wash moved up his arms quickly, and a look of panic flickered across his face just before it froze. As the marble reached the top of his head, it began to crumble. Starting at his crown and moving downward, just as quickly as he'd frozen, he turned to dust.

June's hands shook as she raised one, reaching to warn the nurse that held the child. It was too late. As she placed the bundle on June's lap, she was gone, frozen in time for a split second before crumbling to dust, her remains mixing with the doctor's. June looked down at the infant, barely registering the pink hat, and began to cry.

"June? June!"

A voice pierced her eardrums and a hand yanked the back of her neck. The hospital room she was sitting in moved away from her, or rather, she was pulled from it by the collar of her dress. She watched as the image faded, dark taking over instead. Moments later, she gasped as water splashed around her. The inky blackness she'd moved through faded, and she blinked and sputtered as the obsidian room came back into focus. She raised her head and looked up to see Henry holding her.

She threw her arms around him and sobbed. "I'm sorry, so sorry!"

He gave her a tight squeeze before pulling her away, concern obvious on his face. "What were you doing? You could have drowned!"

She looked down and realized her hair and blouse were soaked in water from the bowl. The surface of what was left in the container was still, but water speckled the cloth around it. She shook her head. "I think I fell over. I'm not sure."

Henry jerked his chin down and looked behind him. June breathed a sigh of relief as she noticed the door was open.

"We have to move quickly," he said.

She grasped his hand and they ran through the big outer room together. He let go of her as they reached the front. Taking her face in his hands, he kissed her hard and fast.

"You have to go," he said. "Poseidon thinks I'm on his side. I have to stay."

June blanched at him. "I thought you were taken!"

Henry nodded. "But I don't trust him, and I don't want to work with him. You have to understand how overwhelming this whole situation is. I didn't run away because I thought it might be good for one of us to be on the inside."

June pulled away and eyed him suspiciously, remembering the image of Henry and Don laughing together. "Are you telling the truth?" she asked.

Henry looked frantic. "Of course! I thought about it a lot. I want to help. I care about you." His eyes were pleading, and June's expression softened. He looked behind him again and stepped back. "I have to go. Don't trust anyone, and talk to Typhon about the void."

Henry turned and ran, bolting across the parking lot like his life depended on it. June stood, dumbstruck, in the doorway of the crumbling building. Void? Poseidon had said that. Could she trust Henry? What if he'd been with Poseidon all along? No, there was no way.

She began to pick her way back toward the main street. She stopped on the sidewalk and turned to look at the building, but the heavy air of the barricade threw a sick feeling over her. She shook her head and stepped away.

She needed Typhon. Her mind was racing, and he was the only being, god or mortal, that could be trusted. She rushed home as quickly as possible, yelling Typhon's name at every breeze that passed.

34

June paced in her living room, jumping at every gust of wind that hit her window frame. Finally, as the sun began to dip below the horizon, her window blew open. She sighed loudly and ran to the leaves that fell into her kitchen. She threw her arms out in the same moment Typhon materialized, and they hugged each other hard. June began to cry and swore. She was crying so much lately. What was wrong with her!

Typhon hugged her tightly and only released her when her shoulders stopped shaking. He stepped back and clapped his hands.

"So, no luck with transporting Henry?" June's face fell, and Typhon's expression softened. "What is it, June-bee?"

June explained that Henry had been taken as collateral as well, and then got her out of the locked room and went back to Poseidon.

Typhon's face looked vaguely horrified. "He's working with him now?"

June shook her head. "I'm not sure. He said to get to you and ask about the void." Ty's face drained of color. "What? What is it?" she asked.

He cleared his throat loudly and leaned against the counter. "While Olympus is all good things, the void is where criminals are sent. Some of the original titans were shoved in there." He swallowed hard. "Thankfully Zeus needed me for something, so I stayed. But once you go in, you do not come out."

"How do you get there?" June chewed her bottom lip.

Typhon shook his head. "It's hard to explain. We call it a void, but it's more like a vortex." He reached out a hand and she took it. "I'll show you."

They turned together and, as if they weighed nothing more than a leaf, caught a breeze that pulled them up and through the kitchen window. They moved quickly, climbing higher and higher in the sky. Once the buildings beneath them looked like specks, their breeze suddenly expanded, then pulled together quickly, snapping on itself like a rubber band, and the world melted away.

When June looked down again, they were above Olympus. As they drifted down, she caught a glimpse of the marble building from above, and her breath caught. It was massive. Gold ceilings stretched for miles in every direction. Large openings in the gold revealed smaller buildings inside the enclosed city. Typhon took them down into the main hall and they materialized in the middle of the room. It had been fixed quickly, and nicely. It looked brand new. June landed on her feet and looked around, surprised to see that no one was in the room. Typhon took off toward a hall at the end of the room, and June had to jog to catch up.

"Where is everyone?" she asked.

Typhon shrugged. "Probably in their rooms. It's pretty late here. We work on a different time wave than mortals."

June nodded and continued following him.

They walked down a grand hall, also marble with gold patterns above them. The hall broke into a massive cathedral-style room with multiple paths, and Typhon chose one of the three to their left. They continued weaving like that, and at the third intersection of entries, the floor began sloping down. June was confused but said nothing as they descended. The marble walls started to get darker, and once they started down a steep decline, the walls turned to gray slate. Typhon reached back and took June's hand, pushing forward into the darkness.

After nearly twenty minutes of walking, June was out of breath and had a stitch in her side. Finally, Typhon took one last turn to the right, and they stopped at the end of a short hallway. It was dark, with only a small bit of light coming from a sconce on the wall. A dark obsidian door stood in front of them, barely large enough for one person to squeeze through.

Typhon turned to June. "Whatever you do, do not touch it. Don't look too far into it either. It's easy to succumb to its call."

June's hands trembled and her stomach flipped as Typhon reached in front of her and swung the door open wide. Inside were walls of black, just like Poseidon's prophecy room, but instead of candles in the corners and a table in the center, a large ball floated a few feet from June. It had the same look as the star-spotted blackness that June fell through in her dreams. It somehow felt cold and warm at the same time, and she felt the urge to reach out and touch it.

"This is the void," Typhon whispered.

June took a step forward, and a silky voice caressed her mind.

Hello child. You've come to meet me in person this time.

She stumbled backward and stared into the center of the void as it spoke.

What help have you come to seek? Or have you instead come to take a step into the unknown?

June reached a hand toward the ball and a shiver went down her spine. A spark of light emitted from the orb and raced up her finger, disappearing on the back of her hand.

"What are you?" she asked, voice barely above a whisper.

I have many names. But, I prefer Chaos.

June nodded before swallowing hard. "I think I'm looking for a way to get rid of Poseidon."

Heavy silence filled the room as the darkness throbbed and grew around her. Finally, the silk slid across the back of her mind again.

I can take him. Bring him to me and he will be with the rest.

"Rest? Rest of what?" Her voice seemed to meld with the black tendrils that had begun to wrap around her body. She was Chaos. Chaos was her. The stars grew brighter.

The rest of the . . . disposed.

June inhaled and her lungs felt as if they were filled with cold starlight. Just as she felt on the verge of free-falling through the ink, a pair of hands on her shoulders yanked her backward, hard.

"June! What are you doing?"

The black fog around her disappeared and she was standing in front of the obsidian door again. She exhaled and her breath felt like fire in her throat.

"What do you mean?" Her words almost choked her.

Typhon spun her around and inspected her. "You were stepping straight in. What were you doing?"

June exhaled again, the spinning in her head beginning to slow. "I was talking with it. Didn't you hear?"

Typhon shook his head, concern obvious. "You didn't say anything. You just kept shuffling closer and closer."

June looked down and studied her hands. "I–I don't understand."

Typhon grabbed her hand and pulled her away from the door, out into the hallway. She leaned against the cold marble, enjoying the sensation on the back of her neck, and slid to the floor.

"Chaos said it'll take Poseidon. I just have to bring him." She looked up at Typhon, anxious. "But how?"

Typhon crouched in front of her, brow furrowed. "It has a name?" He rubbed the spot between his eyebrows and pinched the bridge of his nose. "Never mind. You need to learn to shift. Clearly, you did it in your dreams, but we need to figure out how to do it for real." He held out a hand, which June accepted, and he pulled her to stand and walk with him. "What exactly did it say?"

"Bring Poseidon, and Chaos will take him. It also . . . knew me. It said I came to meet in person this time."

Typhon nodded. "So your dreams have been real."

June stopped and turned to face him. "I've been through Chaos before. I fell through it both times that I left Olympus. I fell straight through and then back home."

Typhons brow furrowed. "I'm not sure what that means."

"It also said that Poseidon would be with the rest—with the disposed."

Typhons spine stiffened and his walk slowed. "The other titans. We didn't know where they actually *went* after going into the void." He turned to her with a serious look on his face. "Did it tell you?"

She shook her head. "No, just that he would be with them."

Typhon resumed the climb from the lower level of the void, June on his heels. "But that he would *be*. Which tells me that they still exist . . ." He trailed off and went silent for the rest of the walk. June followed, lost in her own thoughts about jumping from Earth to here.

They wove through the maze of Olympus together until Typhon stopped in front of a gilded door. He reached out a hand and pressed it to the engraved surface, and it melted away at his touch. June's jaw dropped in shock as she followed him in.

A sitting room greeted them, decorated in shades of tan and orange. It looked as if the entire season of autumn had exploded over the walls and furniture. June stopped in the middle of the room, and Typhon kept going, walking through an arch near the back of the room. He returned after a few seconds holding two large mugs with steam rising from them.

He motioned to one of the couches and June perched on the edge of it, still gawking. He chuckled and handed her a mug, which she accepted gratefully. The smell of pumpkin and chocolate rose with the steam and her mouth began watering.

"What is this?"

Typhon raised his glass and took a drink before answering. "My favorite drink."

June smiled. "I meant this place. Where are we?"

Typhon set the cup down and spread his arms wide. "My apologies. Welcome to my home. Or, what is my home when I'm in Olympus."

"Wow," was all June could say. She raised the cup to her lips and warmth filled her as she drank. It was the best thing she had ever tasted. Pumpkin, cinnamon, and chocolate somehow intertwined perfectly and danced across her tongue. A hint of richer spices and black tea followed the symphony, and she closed her eyes and moaned out loud. "This is so GOOD!"

Typhon laughed and winked at her. "There are some perks to being able to come here." He cleared his throat. "Speaking of which—I think we should start by trying to travel between rooms first."

June blanched at him. "Just like that?"

Typhon nodded firmly. "There's not a second to waste. We get an advantage with time passing faster here than in the mortal realm, but if you're to face Poseidon and get rid of him soon, we need to get to work."

June nodded and set her mug down, and the pair rose together.

"Now, we aren't sure if it's your ability or the baby's, so this may take some trial and error. I want you to envision yourself leaving this spot and appearing there." He pointed to the arch behind him. "Shifting is what us gods do to hop around. You've seen me do it plenty, when I ride the wind. Asclepius has too — theirs is collapsing into scales. It varies between us. Apollo disappears into a blink of bright light and essentially travels through beams of sun."

She nodded and closed her eyes, picturing herself zooming over to the arch and opening her eyes to see the living room from the five feet away that it was. She repeated the image on loop, bracing herself and clenching every part of her body possible. Typhon said something but she ignored it and focused on moving. She felt her body shake a bit and her eyes snapped open from excitement.

She was still in the same spot. Her face fell and Typhon offered her a reassuring smile.

"It's okay, you normally do this in your sleep so it'll be a lot harder now."

June nodded and tried again. This time sweat beaded on her forehead.

Hours passed like that, with June closing her eyes and straining to move herself with her mind, and Typhon encouraging her every time she opened them again. Finally, she sighed. Her face and neck were drenched with sweat, and her legs felt weak. She collapsed onto the couch.

"It's no use, Ty. I can't do it."

Typhon moved to crouch next to her. "It's okay, you will get there, I promise." He looked up and noticed the opening in his ceiling was dark. "Let's eat something and try a different method."

June nodded in agreement.

35

After dinner, they practiced until Apollo began to lift the sun. June's entire body was slick with sweat, and Typhon looked exhausted. They had tried everything from forcing the shift to meditating to June hovering on the edge of sleep and imagining moving. Nothing worked. At one point they thought that she may have shifted a couple of inches, but June was sure she'd simply taken a small step by accident.

As they lounged on the couch together, June's head in Typhon's lap and him dozing against the wall, a sudden loud bang shook the house. June jolted, sitting upright and grabbing Typhon's hand. They looked around together. Silence filled the room until a large black cloud drifted over the hole in the ceiling. It looked menacing, with lightning arcing through it and lighting up various spots with blues and purples. June looked up in awe, and Typhon set his mouth in a grimace. He opened it to speak and a booming voice filled the air around them, cutting him off.

"PO-SEI-DON! HOW DARE YOU!" The voice shook June to her core. She gripped Typhon's hand and blinked, trying to swallow the fear. When she opened her eyes again, they were outside. Typhon and June stared at each other in shock.

"Did you . . .?" she asked.

He shook his head. The boom sounded again, and June ducked involuntarily.

She looked up, and the blood drained from her face. Above them stood a hundred-foot Zeus. He moved slowly but looked terrifying nonetheless. Clouds floated around his head, arced with lightning, and she realized that the boom was the thunder emanating from his steps. His skin was purple, with lightning bolts flashing through his veins. He looked down and she nearly fainted when she saw his face. Where wrinkles were previously, hot electricity outlined his eyes. His beard glowed, and his eyes were white. If Chaos' star-filled blackness was turned inside out, it would have been Zeus' eyes.

He turned back ahead and took another step past Olympus. June followed his path with her eyes and finally saw what was happening.

Hundreds of bright-red creatures were flying toward them. With four unsettling eyes, feathered skin in shades of red and pink, and strong large wings sprouted from their muscular shoulder blades, they looked terrifying, and familiar.

She pointed and yelled over the loud crackling coming from Zeus. "Those attacked me in Spades! What are they?"

"They used to run wild, before Poseidon's minions stole them. They once were Gryphons. Poseidon has had someone change them into absolutely terrible things."

June nodded and turned back to the scene. Zeus raised a hand and lightning arced from his fingertips, blowing down at least twenty of the red creatures. Typhon took her hand and began pulling her away.

"Come on, we shouldn't be here for this. You're not safe."

June pulled her hand back. "But I want to help!"

Typhon turned on her. "You can't help, June! You have a mission. You're not risking your life for Olympus when we won't have anything left if you don't get rid of Poseidon!"

June stepped back, a horrified look on her face. "Why is it up to me to get rid of him? It's your fight! I should get to choose where to participate. I can't even shift, which is the one thing I have to do to beat him. Why don't you do it?"

Typhon sighed and crossed his arms. "You *can* shift! You just did. And there are rules in place for us. We aren't allowed."

June's face heated. "You're all just cowards!"

As if Zeus was cheering for her, another boom clapped through the air around them as she yelled. She turned toward the fight, but mid-spin, she blinked.

When she opened her eyes, the air was still, and she was looking at the obsidian door that led to Chaos. She grumbled and looked around. Unsure if Typhon sent her here or if she brought herself, she stepped up and swung the door open wide. Why here of all places? It was good practice for Poseidon, but was there a point if she couldn't control it? Chaos greeted her with silence. Anger filled her then, followed by discomfort, anxiety, and sadness, each in its own wave. She'd just yelled at her only friend left, as she was unsure if Henry stood with her or not.

Yes, you have a habit of making trouble out of nothing.

She stepped forward.

It's okay, young one, I have a resting place for you.

Black tentacles caressed her and she stepped forward once more, falling face-first into the starlight-speckled ink.

36

The bed that Helen was tied to was as hard as rocks, and she swore every time she tried to shift her weight. She was too damn old for this nonsense. She rolled her hips side to side to try and relieve the pain in them. As she stretched back, a sliver of light popped into existence across the room. She bolted upright and held her breath as Pius walked in.

"Are you going to let me go now?" she asked.

Asclepius set a plate down at the end of the bed and began to slowly shuffle out. As they reached the door, they stopped for a minute, as if they thought of offering some kind words.

"Let me go home!"

Helen's voice made Asclepius flinch, and they turned and looked at her sadly. "I'm sorry. I have orders."

A wrangled cry of despair forced its way up Helen's throat, and she choked back the following sob. "Please. I thought we were good together. I didn't realize what I was getting myself into. I'm sorry."

A look full of hurt flickered over Asclepius' face as they turned back to her. "You really don't know why you're here, do you?"

Helen shook her head, wringing her fingers together. They looked over their shoulder before swinging the door behind them and walking toward Helen.

"This isn't you, Hel. William dug himself a deep hole. You're just collateral."

Helen shook her head, refusing to believe it. "I know he owes money. I thought that was it."

Asclepius reached out to take Helen's hand and she flinched back. Their arm fell awkwardly to their side and they sighed. "He tried to kill Don. William branded your family when he did that."

Helen looked up in shock. William was violent, but not that violent. Right? Asclepius gave her a sad look and turned to leave again.

"Wait! How long will I be here?"

The snake god shrugged. "Until William comes to pay his debt."

Helen's jaw dropped. "But—" Her plea was cut off by the door slamming. Shit. William was dead. He was never going to come. Was she going to die here? She began to sob helplessly. She'd never see her girl again.

37

June blinked, but the darkness around her was the same whether her eyes were open or closed. She felt weightless. Her arms and legs were gone, and she had no heartbeat pounding in her chest. She simply was, and wasn't, at the same time.

Where am I? Her thought left her in a small crumble of light and whizzed around until it sputtered out and faded.

Chaos. The answer wasn't so much spoken as whispered into the very essence of the liquid night that encased her consciousness.

How did I get here? Her words once again balled into a speck of starlight and zigzagged around for a moment.

You walked. The words caressed June and her essence warmed with the feeling of amusement around her.

Why am I here?

Silence followed her question, and the stars began to blink out of existence one by one.

June began falling then. Down into a pit of blackness, she fell for hours. Or maybe it was seconds. Finally, the rush of air around her stopped, and she floated around a large metal cage. Inside were terrifying-looking creatures. Some had fifty heads and even more arms, some had multiple eyes, and all were massive, sweat-covered, and muscled.

Who – June's question was cut off by a hiss from Chaos.

Disposed.

June stayed silent and watched as the beings ambled about their small space. This would be Poseidon's fate then.

She forced herself to look away, unsure how it was possible when she couldn't feel her body. How was she meant to learn how to shift, get Poseidon here, and not get sucked in?

Chaos enveloped her once more and it felt almost as if it were laughing with its entire essence. *You use your fear, child.*

What? What does that mean? Being afraid will help? Stars swirled around her in acknowledgment, but no more words came.

38

June opened her eyes to the ceiling of her bedroom and breathed deeply. The darkness faded from the edges of her vision as she sat up and looked around, surprised to see that nothing had changed, even though she felt as if it had.

She got out of bed and moved downstairs. As she grabbed her sunglasses from the table by her bed, she glanced at herself in the mirror. She looked much better than she had in recent weeks. The bags under her eyes were gone and her face held a bit more color now.

As she rounded the corner to her living room, she stopped dead in her tracks. The couch cushions were on the floor, the pictures on her wall were knocked askew, and muddy boot prints decorated her rug. Her heart rate sped up and she reached for a bat by the doorway, raising it and poising to swing as she walked through to the kitchen. Her apartment looked to be in a similar state as her mother's house was after the suits had ransacked it.

Her tea kettle was in the middle of the kitchen floor, handle gone. The tins that normally held her sugar and flour were missing their lids, and nearly every cabinet was open. She set the bat down once she was sure no one was there and looked over the dining room. Her notebook was missing, as was a small jar that housed her savings. She swore. Of course they would come and take what they wanted. Why they didn't search her room, she had no idea. And why the notebook? Her heart raced. Maybe Henry had told them that that's where she'd written her plans. Gods, how she wished she knew what else was driving this debt collection. She would have just paid it and been done. But she had a feeling this now went much deeper than money.

She did her best to clean up the ransacked rooms and then sat down with her head in her hands. It was early evening, but she didn't feel hungry.

How could her father cause such a mess? She wondered if it would be different if she hadn't turned him. Surely not.

She stood suddenly, remembering the shop. What if they'd taken money from there too? Oh no. Oh no!

She raced downstairs to the gallery as fast as possible, bursting in and looking around quickly. She breathed a sigh of relief. Nothing was out of place. They hadn't come here. To be sure, she walked to the register and clicked it open. Her cash was still in place, and the register itself had a light coating of dust.

She placed her hand on her chest and breathed deeply. This issue with Poseidon was cutting too close into her personal life. If they took her money or destroyed her statues, she would be forced into homelessness.

June rounded the counter and stood in front of her father.

"This is your fault," she whispered.

Suddenly, she was filled with rage. It welled up inside her and hot angry tears began to race down her face. She grabbed the bat and in one smooth move, spun and swung it around at her father.

"How could you do this to us!" she screamed, and the head of the bat connected with William's chest.

Time seemed to slow down as June realized what she'd done. The middle of William's body burst out behind him. Small pieces of white marble with gray veins showered the floor. William's top half began to fall.

June screamed and leaped to catch it, but she was too late. Her father's top, from head to chest, fell and shattered on the floor. The loud crash echoed around her and she dropped to her knees, hands still outstretched.

She cried in earnest then, tears staining his crumbled remains. "Why, Dad?" she choked out. She wished Typhon were here, or Henry. She couldn't remember the last time she had seen them. She sniffed and looked up. Where *were* they? Why was she alone in this?

She stood and looked down at her father's remains. It was all his fault. She knew that. But she couldn't help but blame herself as well. She was alone because she kept chasing away the good people in her life.

She knew what she had to do. Typhon was right; she could shift on her own, and she would.

She made her way from the gallery and back up to her living room. She took a deep breath and sat in the middle of the floor. She conjured the image of the room she'd seen her mother in and breathed deeply. Move, move, move, she thought. She felt the floor shift underneath her and ignored it, picturing the damp, dark walls of her mother's cell. As a bit of cold seeped into her bones, she cracked her eyes open. She was still in her living room.

She swore.

She tried again, and after another infuriatingly unsuccessful attempt, she thought about Chaos.

Fear, it had said. Use her fear.

She closed her eyes and tried to remember how that dank cell-like room had smelled, although she was only there for a few moments. She imagined the sliver of light that appeared when the door opened and the feel of the hard mattress on the floor. The air around her cooled again, and she felt as if half of her was in her living room and half somewhere else. She heard a loud bang outside, and cold fear dropped into the pit of her stomach. Panic filled her and her throat tightened. She opened her eyes, gasping, and saw that she was in the middle of the cell.

She scrambled up and looked around, her eyes adjusting slowly in the pitch black. "Mom?" she whispered.

A loud bang sounded from behind her.

"June?" Helen's voice was hoarse, barely scraping its way to June's ears. She rushed to the source of the voice and fell into her mother's lap. Tears fell freely and her mother stroked her hair.

"How did you get here?" Helen asked, sounding as if she was also crying.

June looked up but couldn't see her face. "It's a long story. I've come to take you home."

Helen laughed, and June sat back, confused. "Mom?"

The laugh warped and twisted until it was clearly no longer her mother's. Under the strange laugh, she could hear rustling behind her, but she could see nothing.

June felt bile rise up in the back of her throat. Suddenly, lights flickered to life around her, and she blinked to force her eyes to focus. Poseidon sat behind her mother on the bed, a hand over Helen's mouth and his legs on either side of her body.

"Hello, June. Nice to see you."

He loosened his grip on her face and ran a thumb on her mouth, and heat rose into June's cheeks. She scrambled back and clenched her fists. "Let her go!"

Poseidon raised a finger from his other hand and wagged it at her. "Tsk. Haven't you learned anything? You need to come here with your father. Tell him to quit hiding and come face me like the man he is—or is supposed to be." He gave her a sickening grin and her stomach turned to a block of ice. He stood, shoving her mother to the side, and approached June, crouching in front of her.

"My father is—" Her words were cut off as he reached out a finger and placed it in the middle of her forehead.

"See you soon," he hissed, shoving her back.

She fell, slamming into her body on her living room floor and left gasping for air. She blinked fast and shot to her feet, lurching forward to catch her balance only to slam into a hard body. She looked up and the breath was knocked from her as a large hand shoved into her chest and pushed her back. She stumbled backward but stayed upright, and it took a moment for her vision to clear. She looked up to see one of the suits standing where she had just been. Gods, why did they all look the same? She glared at him, and it took a moment to register that he was wearing sunglasses.

"What do you want?" she asked, trying to make her voice sound angry, but she was sure there was a squeak in it.

"Here to collect you and William." He grunted and stepped forward. June dodged his arm as he reached out to grab her, and she sidestepped into the kitchen.

"Oh, you want my dad?" An idea formed in her mind and she smiled coyly at the suit. "He's downstairs. Let's go get him."

She turned and ran through the kitchen, grabbing the doorframe to swing herself down the step. She bounded down, the suit ambling after her, and she ran to the gallery door as fast as possible. She stumbled into the room and ran behind the remains of her father, his hips coming up to her waist. She poised herself there, grinning as the suit walked in and stood in the door. She spread her arms wide.

"Here he is. Hey, Dad, meet one of the idiots trying to take me." She reached down and picked up a large chunk of William's back, heaving it as hard as she could at the man in the suit. He looked surprised as it spun toward his face, hitting him square in the nose. He threw his hands up to his face, and his glasses fell off. June ran straight toward him then, reaching up to ball her fist around his tie and pull him down before he could recover himself. She held him, hunched over, and looked him in the eye.

Once he was stone, it took a moment to loosen her hand from the wrinkled gray she'd grabbed onto — the marble had formed around her fingers. She yanked hard and freed her hand, and she laughed at the mark in the statue. She looked at her nails and her laugh faded. Gray dust was under her nails. Her mind raced as she imagined scratching someone's skin and pulling it with her hands. Bile rose in her throat and she shook her head to try and clear the image.

She forced a breath in and out and walked over to her father. If Poseidon wanted both of them to show up, then they would. She bent down and picked up his hand, which had miraculously broken off at the wrist and stayed whole. Unwrapping her scarf, she carefully placed the piece in the fabric and began digging through the rest of the rubble until she found a large chunk of William's face. It only held part of his forehead, his eye, his cheek, and the right side of his mouth, but it would be enough.

She gingerly traced a finger down his cheek and whispered, "I'm sorry, Dad." She set it next to the hand and wrapped both pieces tightly in the scarf, then tucked them into her pocket. She stood and wiped a tear from her cheek and closed her eyes, focusing on the outside of the gallery. The air thrummed around her, and she clenched her eyes tighter, focusing on the smell of the road outside and the coil of fear in her stomach. It had rained earlier, so she knew it would hold the smell of wet dirt and grass, and there would be a mild breeze. She pictured the terror that gripped her when she was chased by suits. She didn't open her eyes until she felt the cold air nip at her nose and found herself outside the diner door.

She smiled to herself and began walking down the road, forcing a shift every few feet. After she traveled a few blocks this way, she knew she was ready. All it took was a bit of anger and letting the cold of panic seep into her bones enough to force her mind to jump.

June closed her eyes again and imagined Olympus. One last visit.

It took a few tries, and some strange looks from people walking past her, but finally June opened her eyes and found herself in the marble hall. The sun shone above her, just like that first visit, and she looked around. Surprisingly, large marble chairs were surrounding the center, where none had been what seemed like an hour before. Seated in a few of them were Zeus, Typhon, Apollo, and who she could only assume were Hera and

Aphrodite, based on the fact one sat next to Zeus and the other was more beautiful and radiant than anyone she'd ever seen. She blinked, and they all stared at her in silence for a moment before Typhon descended, a large grin on his face. He shrunk as he stepped down from the throne, holding his arms out to give her a quick hug. June squeezed him, relieved to see that he was okay after the attack by Poseidon's creatures.

"You got here on your own?" he asked, seemingly thrilled.

June smiled and nodded. "I figured it out. It just took some practice—and a bit of Chaos."

Typhon cocked his head at that and the corner of his mouth tugged up.

Zeus cleared his throat and June turned to face him.

"It's time, I think," she said. "I came to practice getting to Chaos. Do you mind if I borrow Ty?"

Zeus smiled and inclined his head before turning back to Hera and saying something about Kansas. June didn't try to listen. She faced Typhon and held out a hand.

"Ready?" she asked. He nodded. She closed her eyes and pictured Chaos—the swirling black speckled with bright stars and the cold feel of him. She imagined herself appearing next to it, and opened her eyes when Zeus' voice faded away. They were outside the obsidian door. Typhon looked a bit sick. She gave him an inquisitive look, and he shook his head.

"I'm fine. It's strange to have someone else do the shift."

June nodded and looked at the door. "I wanted us to come next to it, not outside the room."

Typhon furrowed his brow. "Maybe we should leave the door open?"

"Can't it get out then?"

Typhon shook his head. "No, there's a lot of protection in place to prevent that. Let's try again." He stepped up and opened the door, making sure to swing it wide open, and then stepped up to June again. She took his hand and spun them back into the great hall. Zeus raised an eyebrow at them, to which June returned a sheepish smile. She shook out her hands before placing one on Typhon's shoulder and whisking him away again. This time, she managed to get them within inches of Chaos. Typhon stumbled away from it quickly, pulling her with him, and June patted his arm to reassure him.

"It's okay, I've gone in and out of it multiple times now. If it wanted to keep me, it would."

Typhon still looked uneasy.

They clasped hands and began to walk up the hall, and Typhon took a moment before asking, "So, you've figured out how to get to Chaos. What now?"

June smiled. "Now, we end this."

He nodded and spun, taking them both to just outside Olympus in a flurry of leaves.

"I'll let everyone know not to touch that door, and I'll rally the forces in case he brings an army. You just focus on getting Poseidon here and on not getting hurt." He held both her shoulders and looked her in the eye. She nodded.

"I'll be okay, I promise." With that, she spun away, disappearing into darkness.

39

June materialized on forty-second street, with the sun shining brightly above her. That had to be a good omen, right? She peeked around the corner and could see the decrepit building that Poseidon was hiding in. She grimaced and turned back around, patting her pockets to make sure the pieces of her father were still there. She looked up, thinking it was around ten am, and smiled. That slip of paper had said noon, so maybe she would catch him by surprise. She breathed deeply and turned the corner, pulling her forgotten sunglasses from the neck of her dress and slipping them onto her face.

Approaching the invisible wall took more willpower than she thought she had. Sickness came over her as she took a step in, and all the bad memories she held deep in her mind surged up.

Another step, and bile bit at her tongue.

Another step, and dizziness overtook her.

She clenched her teeth and forced herself forward, thinking of her mother who had been held captive, and Henry. Oh, Henry, how she hoped he was truly on her side.

One final step, and she came out of the haze. She stopped once she was clear of the wall and bent down, retching up stomach acid. It took a few minutes to recover herself, and once she stopped heaving, she stood and shot the shimmery air a dirty look. How could an invisible barrier cause her so much pain? She righted her dress and looked at the building in front of her.

This place really felt abandoned. Bits of the walls were crumbled, and every window seemed to be coated in a thick layer of grime. There was no sign of life anywhere, save for two rats sniffing a puddle of some murky substance under a broken pipe to her right. She took a step forward, and they scurried off.

She kept walking. Halfway to the building, she watched three suits step out from the front door. They looked like the same ones from the factory. All three moved in uniform, pacing in front of the door. They didn't seem to notice her yet, so she quickly looked around, spotted a stack of disposed tires, and ran to duck behind them. She didn't know how it would go if she had to turn three men at once. She was already exhausted. She wasn't even sure when she'd last slept. The days had morphed together after flipping between here and Olympus so much. She forced herself to breathe and steady her heart rate. It would be okay. Maybe she could distract them somehow. She patted her skirt down and realized that she didn't have anything with her to use as a distraction, and there was nothing around her either. She didn't want to have to turn them all at once if she didn't have to, then face Don immediately after. Gods knew what else was waiting for her before she even reached him. She was tired as it was. She could only see one option—to try and separate them. She'd run up and get them to chase her in order to break them apart so she could turn them one by one, like at the bar. Maybe she could even lead one back through the magic wall.

She crept from her hiding place and looked up. The suits continued to pace. She bolstered herself and walked toward them with purpose. Twenty feet away, they still didn't look at her. Ten feet.

"Hey!" she yelled.

The three stopped together and turned sharply. She stopped walking, and they all stared at each other. She took a step forward, and the one in the middle smiled as the other two moved to flank her. Their suits began to bubble. June stepped back. Oh no.

The ties around their necks turned a deep shade of brown and their bodies began melting together. Their suits grew into massive scales the size of dinner plates, and they grew until they stood at least fifteen feet tall. June took another step back, heart pounding, and looked up. Three sets of eyes stared down at her, set on top of pointed heads. A low hissy growl started deep in the creature's chest. She stepped back again. The creature's three tongues flicked out, and a bit of green venom dripped from the one on the left, forcing her to stumble back. The drop of venom fell to the ground where her feet had been and sizzled in the mud, causing a rancid-smelling puff of smoke to rise.

Air whooshed out of her lungs as she looked into the middle head's eyes, and she realized that she was staring up into the face of a hydra.

"Stand down." She tried to project her voice as much as possible.

The massive three-headed reptile opened its center mouth and let out a deafening roar that shook the ground beneath them before it whipped all three of its heads down to look at her. Her mind raced as she tried to remember what hydras could do. It had been years since she'd read a story about one in school.

In a panic, June reached up and pulled her glasses off to look into his eyes. The center head froze and let out a pained sound as the stone chased itself across his neck. In mere seconds, the large hellish monster's head was white marble. She grinned triumphantly as she turned her gaze to the one to the left. As the gray wash started turning the scales of its jaw, the center stump of a neck began to tremble. June stepped back and dove behind a pile of broken pallets as a spurt of green goo shot into the air and showered over where she had just been standing. She looked down at her dress and swore at the fabric that was eaten through by a splash of the stuff. She peeked up over the pile of wood and nearly choked from shock.

Where the center head had broken off, two scaly vines were lurching up through the stone. Bile rose in her throat as more venom spewed and two heads regrew in its place, faster than even her marble could run its course.

She swore again as she realized the same was happening to the other head on the right, and in mere seconds, the creature had five long necks, and all sets of eyes turned on her hiding place.

With a massive hiss, the head on the left reared up, its neck swelling, before it shot a stream of goo at her. She ran as hard as she could, narrowly avoiding the acidic slime that fell behind her. She threw herself behind another pile of tires and tried to catch her breath, huffing heavily with a hand on her chest. Stone was not going to work on this thing if it was going to regrow heads. She looked around and spotted a long, broken pipe a few feet away.

A quick glance behind her showed the monster pacing. It turned back toward the door and she sprung up. She whipped the pipe upward, grunting at its weight, and threw herself into a run toward the creature. As she reached it, a tail swept toward her and she jumped, tripping over her feet and falling to the ground. Stars blinked into her vision and her heart caught in her throat as the creature began shrinking and turned toward her. As its tail wrapped around itself and six arms sprung out of its chest, she leaped forward, thrusting the rusty end of the pipe into its chest.

The creature let out a shriek loud enough to rattle the windows in the building, and she shoved the pipe in further, throwing all her weight against it. All five sets of eyes turned down on her and she glared up, catching each one and watching the marble race up its necks as purple blood spurted from its chest. A drip of venom fell from the head on her right and she screamed and fell back as it burned her eye.

She scrambled across the ground backward with a hand slapped to her face and tears prickling her other eye, trying to keep it open to watch as the scaly necks writhed around and threw themselves sideways, unbalanced on half-turned human legs.

The creature continued to scream as June crawled to a puddle of water to the left. She scooped some of the muddy substance into her hand and threw it at her eye, biting her scream of pain back as she gasped. The pain was unlike anything she'd ever experienced, and she kept trying to wash out the venom until it faded to a dull thud.

The sounds of thrashing stopped behind her, and her shoulders shook as she turned. She tried to open the eye that had taken the venom to it and bit her tongue at the effort it took. She covered her good eye and the breath rushed from her body and choked back a cry. She couldn't see anything. The world was dark through her right eye and she tried to hold back a sob as she opened her left and took in the destruction in front of her.

The bottom half of the hydra was slack, with four human legs sprouted around the two scaled ones. Purplish black blood coated its entire body and her eyes trailed up the rest of it. Two of its human arms were missing, and the rest were stone, which had also captured all five of its heads. They were twisted at odd angles, sharp teeth glinting white in the sunlight, and June's fingers shook as she raised them to her face.

She'd felt the power surge up in her from turning the hydra, and now that it was gone, she felt empty and more tired than before. She braced her hands on her knees, allowing herself a moment to rest before standing and walking around the half-stone, clearly dead, monster.

She slid the glasses back on and made her way through the main entrance quickly, eyeing the left set of stairs before deciding on the right. She was thoroughly exhausted, but knew she had to keep moving. As she began to ascend the steps, her nose wrinkled of its own volition. The smell of decay hit her like a bus, and she had to fight past a wave of nausea when it worsened on the next step. She slid over to the right of the stairs and clenched the rail as hard as possible, praying the stairs didn't collapse and fighting to keep her breath steady and ignore the smell of rot as she climbed.

There was nothing but an empty table on the second floor, and another set of steps.

Near the top of the second staircase, she caught the faint whisper of voices above her. She looked up but couldn't make out what they were saying. She crept up the last few steps and came out on yet another empty level, and she stopped. Her heart was pounding, with blood rushing in her ears. *He* was here. Only one more staircase to climb.

She rounded the corner and began her final ascent. On the fourth step, she dropped to her hands and knees and crawled. The metal edge of the steps bit into the palms of her hands, but she ignored it. Five more steps. Three. She stopped at the top. A thin two-foot-wide wall separated her and the men talking on the other side. Her ears perked up as she made out Henry's voice. Suddenly, Poseidon roared with laughter.

Her mind flashed back to the vision in the bowl. Heat rose in her body and her anger surged up. How dare that *disgusting* god laugh at anything. How dare he even feel the right to smile after the terrible things he'd done.

"Yeah, boys, not too long now and we'll have a proper place. Henry is using those connections to fix us up nice."

June faltered at hearing Poseidon's voice. Surely not? It had to be an act.

"How'd you manage to snag this goofball anyway? Seems a bit useless in my opinion." A loud slamming sound reverberated through the air following the stranger's question.

"We don't talk about our interns that way, James. And Henry here simply got an offer he couldn't refuse, isn't that right?" Silence fell before Poseidon laughed. "What was it again, boy? Help me, and you get June?"

The hair on the back of her neck stood on end, and she breathed a sigh of relief. He wasn't against her. A chorus of laughter from the other side of the wall followed Poseidon's statement, and June clenched her jaw. Steeling herself for what was coming, she stepped into the room. She cleared her throat and silence fell.

"Hello, gentlemen."

In the center of the room sat a large round table, with seven rickety-looking seats around it. Poseidon sat in the middle, with five suits around the rest of the table. The undeniable back of Henry's head was facing her, and he stiffened when she spoke. She tried to send a silent thought to him. It's okay.

The man furthest to the left jumped up and yelled, "Oi! Who let the broad in?"

Poseidon laughed and clapped his hands together, standing with a flourish. He faltered as he looked past her, and his hands dropped.

"Where is William?"

June smirked and stepped forward until she was a few feet in front of the table. She fished the bundle of cloth from her pocket, tossing it to Poseidon. She stepped back as he nearly fumbled the package, and she watched with narrowed eyes while he unwrapped it.

"What is this?" He dropped the pieces to the table and glared at her.

"You asked for me to bring my father."

Poseidon looked June up and down. "Grab her." He punctuated his words with a snap and the suit that had insulted her ran around the table.

As he moved toward her, she stepped forward, tearing the glasses from her face and fixing her intense gaze on him. He stopped mid-step and toppled. His shoulder crumbled under the weight of his stone body with a loud crunching sound. His face was contorted into a scream that didn't escape.

"I ain't no broad." June sneered at the dead man and looked up at the rest of the group, fixing her glasses again. The tension in the room was suffocating, and she took another step forward. She forced a laugh out and spread her arms. "So, who wants to go next?"

All at once, the remaining suits shot up. Henry scrambled to the side of the room as chairs scraped the ground loudly, a couple falling with a loud thud. Plumes of dust rose around the men's feet as they bolted around the table. The man to the far right reached June first. He swung his fist hard toward her, and she swiveled, tearing the glasses off her face with one hand, and throwing her other behind her for momentum.

The pair locked eyes and the man fell forward, shattering into pieces. June turned back in time to see the man to Poseidon's left pull out a gun. The last one leaped over the table, reaching for her. His face turned stark white, and he fell through the rickety wood with a loud crash. Splinters and fine dust filled the air, and the cocking sound of a pistol turned June to the last man. He pointed the gun at her, legs braced firmly, and she smirked. She stepped forward and stared into his eyes. He slammed his own shut a second too late, as the marble raced its way up his legs. He froze with his finger on the trigger. June looked down and slid her glasses back on. Her muscles ached, but she felt incredible. Power coursed through her as she stepped up to the remains of the table and looked at Poseidon, who had stood statue-still during the chaos and was looking at her with a strange expression. She couldn't tell if it was fear or confusion, or both.

"Sit down, Don."

He didn't move. She looked to the left of the room, spotting another wooden table, this one long and thin. Atop it was an engraved decanter and six empty whiskey glasses. She smiled, blinked, and appeared next to the table. Out of the corner of her eye, she saw Poseidon reach for his holster, and she tsked at him, turning fully to face him. She pointed at the seat behind him.

"I said *sit*." He raised his hands and obeyed, lowering himself slowly. She glanced at Henry, who stood frozen amidst a pile of rubble, and jerked her head. "Go find my mother, please."

He dipped his chin, terror etched on his face, and ran from the room.

June turned back to the decanter and popped the top off, pouring herself a generous glassful.

Poseidon breathed heavily. "What are you?"

June turned and smirked at him. "Your creation, *Don*."

His face drained of color as he watched her.

"Do you know why I'm here?" Silence filled the room around them as she fixed the stopper again and lifted her glass. She turned to Poseidon and smiled. "I'll tell you. It's not because you asked me. I'm not sure if you noticed, but I came at my own time, of my own free will."

Poseidon scoffed. "You're here because I summoned you. I don't know what game you're playing, girl, but I'm owed a life."

June took a long drink, letting the bitter alcohol burn its way down her throat and spread warmth through her chest and stomach as it went. She walked up to Poseidon and dropped the glass over the remains of the table. It fell and shattered, the brown liquid mixing with white dust to create a puddle among the woodchips.

"You have a life there." She nodded to the half of William's face still clutched in Poseidon's hand. "I'd say our family's debt is settled, wouldn't you?"

Poseidon shook his head, amusement playing on his lips. "No, because *I* didn't take it. I don't know what you think you are, or who, or if you're trying to play gods, or think you hold some power over me, but what I say in this city goes. And the debt is most definitely not settled. Your father owed me thousands as well."

"Well, Donny boy, you're not getting that money back. I'm not sure if it's clicked for you yet, but *I* killed my father. Don't think I won't do the same to *you*."

Poseidon began to stand, and June snatched the marble back from Poseidon, slamming it down onto his leg and hissing, "Sit down."

She braced her hand on the arm of his chair and lowered herself to be eye level with him. "I'm actually not here about the debt. I'm here to tell you a story. Don't worry, it won't take long, and it will answer your questions."

She straightened and grinned at him before stepping away and beginning to pace.

"Once upon a time, there was a cute little restaurant in New York. In that restaurant, a girl worked hard every day. She was fresh out of school with big plans to become an artist! She wanted to be famous and make something of herself. She worked her tail off saving for college, which was to begin soon." She paused and looked at Poseidon, but his expression was unreadable. "One day, a handsome man strode in. His presence captivated her, as did his grandeur stories. His words charmed her and made her believe she was about to experience true love for the first time. He made her trust him. Little did she know, he was there to hurt her."

June stopped her pacing and turned to face him. His knuckles were white from gripping the chair arms. He began to stand, and June let a bit of air hiss between her teeth before she reached down, broke off a piece of one of his lackeys, and threw it as hard as possible at him. He dodged at the last second and she nodded to the chair. With bewilderment on his face, he sat again.

"You see, she skipped her break that day *just* to chat with this wonderful man. He seemed kind, and interesting. Unfortunately, he said he was a smoker. They went outside together so he could have a cigarette. Before the girl knew it, he attacked her."

June walked up to Poseidon and braced her arms on either side of him once more. Her voice dropped to a whisper. "That man shoved her down and had his way with her, tearing her in half and breaking her soul. Do you know who that man was, Don?"

He shook his head, as if denying it could make it less true.

"It was you." She let go of the chair and strode away, walking to the only statue standing and circling him. She inspected his face as she spoke. "Then, believe it or not, you had the audacity to come for my mother, because hurting me to get back at William wasn't enough. So, I'm here to settle things. You came to me for a debt. I'm here to collect what you took from me." She leaned on the frozen man. "What you may not have known is that your crime led to me attaining the wonderful gift of turning pigs like you into debris like that." She spat the words at him and spread her arms out, motioning to the rubble around them.

Gods, she hoped he couldn't see through her bluff.

Poseidon opened his mouth to speak, and June raised a finger to shush him. "I understand how badly you wanted me back then. I want you just as badly now. And luckily for both of us, you'll be with me forever. I've been looking for the perfect piece to stand outside my gallery, you see."

June stepped forward and Poseidon flinched. She moved behind him, tracing her fingers along his shoulder and down his torso. She worked his gun free from its holster and breathed hot air into his ear as she whispered, "I don't like how these look in stone." She rounded the chair to face him again.

"I didn't—" His sentence was cut off by a sharp slap to the face.

"Tsk, tsk, Poseidon. Don't try to lie. You don't think I remember our meetings since? You thought I didn't have the power to stop you." She blinked and shifted to the other side of the room. "Jokes on you. I have help." She shifted back in front of him and laughed.

His face contorted and he tried to rise. She shoved him back down and held her free hand on his shoulder.

"Are you ready?" she asked, mirth filling her voice. She met his eyes and stopped. Was she really going to throw this god into Chaos? She remembered the terrifying monsters it held, and her heart skipped a beat. Yes, he deserves it, she reminded herself.

His face was a mask of pure terror. He clearly didn't know what exactly she was or that she couldn't really hurt him. Not in the way he expected anyway. She grinned and straightened.

"I'll actually give you a choice, as I'm feeling benevolent. Zeus would like a word with you. I'll take you to Olympus and let you face him, instead of decorating my garden."

Poseidon's teeth clenched and he stood, shoving June to the side. "I can get to Olympus on my own," he spat.

June cocked her head. "Can you? Last I heard, you had a life-ban from the city."

He wiped his hand over his face and suddenly lunged at her. June dove away, holding her foot out to trip him. He stumbled past and swore as he caught himself on a broken fragment of table.

June was behind him in an instant, pointing the gun at his back.

He laughed lightly and tried to turn, but she shoved the barrel against his suit harder.

"I'll go willingly to my death if you'll forgive me," he said.

She pushed away from him and swore under her breath. She couldn't trust a god. Well, she could, but not this one. And forgive? He was insane. Poseidon rose behind her, and she turned to face him. He still towered over her, but he somehow seemed smaller than before. He was smiling at her, and something inside June snapped. She whipped around, raising her leg and kicking him in the chest, screaming. He fell to the ground on his back, surprise taking over his features.

"I will NEVER forgive you!" Her voice bounced off the crumbling walls of the room, and he flinched. She planted her feet on either side of his body.

As she reached down to touch his temple, his thick fingers wrapped around her ankles. The familiar niggle of panic started in the back of her mind, and she slammed her eyes shut, picturing Chaos. Poseidon's grip tightened and the air around them trembled for a moment. As all went still, she opened her eyes to see the void a foot away from them.

Poseidon looked around, eyes frantic, before yelling. As the word "No!" left him, a tentacle reached out from Chaos, stretching toward them.

Suddenly, the ground shook and hot electricity zipped through June. She gasped and blinked, and when her eyes opened again, they were back in the room of the abandoned building.

A wave of dizziness took over and she stumbled back, accidentally giving Poseidon the space he needed to scramble up.

Her vision finally cleared and she looked up to see him grinning.

"Bastard," she spat. "What was that?"

He laughed maniacally and stepped toward her. "I'm banned from Olympus, remember." He reached for the holster on his hip and paused as he felt for his gun.

Hot rage burned through June. She was not going to let him leave this room. And he was willing to shoot her? No, this ended here. Her mind went blank as cold anger seeped through every nerve of her body. She was sure her hands were shaking as she cocked the gun, mind devoid of any thoughts.

Poseidon spat at her. "You were weak then and you're weak now."

That was all she needed. One last reason.

She pulled the trigger.

The shot echoed around her, and she watched as blood bloomed on Poseidon's forehead. A thin hole sat between his brows. June stood, frozen in place, staring at that spot as seconds ticked by before his body fell to the floor with a loud thud.

Minutes passed before a pair of hands wrapped around her, causing her to flinch. They pried the gun from her hands in the next moment.

"It's okay," Henry whispered.

She breathed out and relaxed. She felt all her emotions crash down on her and she sagged into

Henry's chest and began crying. She sobbed loud and hard as her anger dissipated and grief took its place. She'd just shot him. She messed up the plan.

She felt Helen's tender hands on her arms then and collapsed with her mother, falling into her lap.

"Mom!"

She cried. She tried to force out words but they escaped her lips in wet gargled bursts, and her mother stroked her hair while Henry rubbed her back. They comforted her for a long while until loud whistles sounded from nearby. The sound grew until it was right outside the building, and June sniffed, sitting up and wiping her tears away.

She looked up at Helen and smiled sadly. "I didn't think I'd get you back," she whispered.

Helen squeezed her hand in response, and Henry cleared his throat.

"We should probably go. I'm sure those are police. The wall is probably down since he's gone."

June nodded and stood, taking both their hands. She had her family back. It would be okay.

"Brace yourselves." She spun, whisking them all away.

40

June took the three of them to Helen's house, although she misjudged slightly and they landed short of the first porch step. June turned to Helen with a grin. Her smile faltered when she noticed that her mother's face looked a bit green. She hooked her arm through Helen's and led her inside, with Henry following close behind.

June flopped on the couch, running her hands over her head. She let out a loud sigh as Helen situated herself on the chair opposite and Henry sat next to her, draping his arm behind her shoulders. She scrubbed her face with her hands, mind running through everything that had happened. As her hands fell from her face, Helen gasped loudly, and June's head snapped up.

"What? What's wrong?"

Helen jumped up and rushed to June, falling on her knees and taking her face in her hands. "Oh, honey . . . your eye!"

June's hand flew up to where the hydra had burned her, and she grimaced. She'd completely forgotten about it in the rush after facing the creature.

"Oh, gods. What am I going to do?"

Helen tsked and rose. "I'll grab a cloth."

June placed her head in her hands as Henry ran a hand up and down her back. She had no idea what she must look like now. She couldn't see through that eye and gods knew what that acidic saliva could do to skin. It had burned like all hell.

"Let me see," Henry said.

His voice broke her train of thought and she groaned. "No."

"Please, June. I'm sure it's not that bad."

She let out a sigh and raised her face. A flicker of emotion passed over Henry's features for a moment, and he touched a finger to her cheek before the corner of his mouth tugged up in a smile.

"You're still gorgeous. It'll be okay."

June sucked on her bottom lip a moment and nodded. There wasn't much that could be done anyway, but he still liked her, even after everything they'd been through.

Helen rushed back around the corner then and gently pressed a warm cloth to June's face, and June smiled her thanks.

"What now?" Helen whispered. She was clearly still shaken, her face pale and her fingers trembling as she clasped her hands in her lap.

June shook her head. "I'm not sure. I-I messed up the plan."

Helen gave her a confused look, and Henry squeezed her shoulder reassuringly before she took a deep breath and prepared to explain everything that Helen had missed during her captivity.

On the cusp of war with a prophetic child joining the family, and fate intertwined with the gods, the adventure is far from over for the Georgians.

Turn the page for a sneak peek of…

THE
OATH
OF EVE

The Violents Book Two

1

June still had vivid dreams, although none were like when she visited Chaos or Olympus. In fact, she had seen neither since her last encounter to lay out the plan to defeat Poseidon, which had failed quite miserably.

Yet, today, she was woken from a dream of Olympus by her water breaking.

In the wee hours of the morning, Henry had helped her gather things to take to the hospital. She'd let her eyes wander over the paintings gifted by her mother that covered their living room, and she'd taken a moment to enjoy the warmth of their kitchen. Theirs. Together.

Even though Henry had purchased this house on his own, together they'd made it into a home through the end of her pregnancy. And once the house had been completely decorated, Henry gifted her with a beautiful engagement ring. They were wed just days earlier.

It hadn't been long before her contractions progressed and pulled her attention away from her reminiscing, but she still couldn't help but think of Typhon as they drove to the hospital.

Her childhood friend had up and vanished. She hadn't heard from him in months. And as Henry helped her waddle through the massive hospital doors, she whispered to the breeze, "Ty, please come."

Labor progressed quickly, and before she knew it, Henry stood to her right, clasping her hand.

"Breathe, June. Breathe. Just one more push!"

The nurse at June's feet echoed the sentiment, and June bore down with all her strength, her scream filling the room.

"Done!" the nurse cried, and the doctor rushed over to take the small pink thing from her.

June smiled weakly and leaned back. Henry clenched June's hand, craning his neck to see past the nurse, before he beamed down at June.

"A girl!" he whispered loudly, voice filled with excitement.

June's smile widened, although she couldn't shake the feeling that something was wrong. This wasn't the vision she'd seen in Poseidon's bowl of prophecy.

She watched warily as the doctor handed the baby to another nurse, who took her to the sink and began to run water for a bath. As the water touched her skin, the infant cried for the first time. The sound shook June to her core and made her want to cry. Thankfully, the scream faded into a quiet burble of sounds after a moment, and June relaxed.

"Evelyn." She turned to look at Henry. "I think we should call her Evelyn."

He smiled and gave her hand a squeeze. She turned her attention back in time to see the doctor remove his gloves. He reached down to touch baby Evelyn, and her tiny fingers grazed his hand. In a split second, the doctor was frozen, stuck into marble with his hand still outstretched to the baby. June sat bolt upright and yelled as pieces of his stone body crumbled off. She stared in horror as the first nurse hurried over to pick up the baby and get her away from the man falling in on himself. She held it to her chest as June stared and Henry covered his mouth.

The newest addition to the Georgian family was like June, but far more powerful.

As June reached out a hand toward the doctor, jaw dropped in shock, a powerful gust of wind threw open the labor ward door. Both June and Henry's heads snapped toward it, and June let out a strangled sound as she tried to move.

"Typhon!"

He was by her in an instant, holding her shoulder so she stayed put. His face was grave, and her wide smile faltered when she noticed fear in his eyes.

"Ty? What's wrong? Where have you been?"

He shook his head sadly and patted June's shoulder once before sweeping toward the nurse. The god placed a hand on the slight woman's shoulder and something in her seemed to change. June watched, confused beyond belief as he leaned in and whispered something in her ear.

"What are you—" June stopped as the woman handed baby Evelyn to Typhon and began to move out of the room. Finally, he turned back to her.

"I'm so sorry, June-bee, but we have to go."

"Go? Go where? Where the hell have you been? And what are you thinking!"

June's fingers began shaking and she held her arms out to take her baby, but Typhon didn't move.

"I'm sorry," he whispered again.

Suddenly, the air around June warped. Everything in her reality seemed to stretch as thin as thread, and in a moment, she was flying through the air. Typhon carried her out of the hospital room window, and she could only turn in time to catch a glimpse of the doctor's stone dust following them before she was thrown upward into a sweeping current of air.

June materialized in the receiving hall of Olympus, standing up. The moment her feet touched the ground, her legs buckled, and a pair of strong hands caught her. She looked up, breathing a sigh of relief as she saw Henry behind her.

It took a moment to orient herself before she finally caught sight of Typhon a few feet away.

"Ty! Give the baby to me. Now."

He shook his head sadly and turned toward a set of twelve pedestals. June recognized them as the same ones that Zeus had sat on with other Olympians the year before. She could barely recall what they had been discussing at the time.

As she looked in the face of the different gods, a lump formed in her throat. All had a grave look, as if an important death had occurred. She tried to squash her rising level of anxiety over the fact that she still hadn't held her child, and she turned her attention to Zeus.

June gathered all the strength she could muster and stepped forward, pointing her finger up at him. "I don't know what you all think you are doing by bringing us here, but I want to leave. Now." She tried her best to keep her tone even and stepped forward again. As she moved, her shaking lessened and she began to feel more normal, as if Olympus itself were lending her energy.

Zeus motioned to Evelyn. "This is the child, the newest Gorgon?"

June opened her mouth to speak, but Henry cleared his throat. "It's—it's actually Georgian. Well, Chekov now."

Zeus raised an eyebrow at him before turning his attention to June. "Well, young one, it seems we have a bit of a situation."

June's face heated. "The only 'situation' is that you cradle-napped my newborn whom I haven't even held yet!"

Zeus held her gaze for a moment before snapping and motioning to Typhon, who walked back to June. He held Evelyn out with an apologetic look, and gently placed her in June's arms. Tears welled in the new mother's eyes as she gazed down at her girl. She was perfect. She had dark hair, like June, but it seemed to be straighter, and her eyes were closed and puffy around the edges. Her cheeks were flushed pink and her bottom lip was pouted out, as if she was about to cry.

Zeus cleared his throat, interrupting June's first moment with her newborn, and she glared at him.

"As you know, you failed to take care of Poseidon. His essence woke on Olympus this morning. We believe he's gone back to New York at this time, but we have no way of knowing if he'll stay there, or what he's up to. We would like you to keep an eye out and intervene if necessary. And then there's the issue of that child."

He motioned to the baby, and June held her protectively. "There is no issue here. She is my child, and she was born less than thirty minutes ago!"

Zeus sighed as if he was tired of the conversation. He glanced at Hera, who had been silently watching.

"As for Poseidon," June said, "perhaps if you'd had the foresight to turn off his exile from Olympus, the plan to throw him into Chaos would have worked! I tried. I really did. But as soon as I got him here, we were thrown out like pieces of paper on the wind. It's not my fault, and not my problem anymore."

June looked around at the other gods, recognizing Apollo, and noticed that all of them looked uneasy.

Hera spoke then. "Juniper . . ." Her voice was kind and warm. "Other issues aside, that baby is Poseidon's. She is immortal and belongs on Olympus. She will grow fast, strong, and powerful. The mortal world is no place to raise her."

"And would we stay here with her then?"

Hera looked uncomfortable as she reached out and held Zeus' hand. "No, dear. Mortals are incapable of surviving for long here. She would stay with us, alone."

June blanched and looked at Typhon helplessly, who was wringing his hands. She swiveled back to Zeus and pointed an accusatory finger at him. "You mean to tell me that you yanked me from a hospital room immediately after labor in order to tell me that you plan to take my child away *and* that her biological father has been set loose on our home city once again? And you want me to take care of him again? You're all *fucking* insane." She spat her last sentence out, and in her peripherals she could see a few gods flinch. She was sure that no one had spoken to Zeus like that in a long time.

He shook his head. "I'm sorry that we took you so suddenly. I'm sure you remember that time passes differently here. It's up to you in the end, Juniper. As you said, she is your child, *but* she is also Poseidon's. Our children have a place here and the community they need to harness their abilities and thrive. Immortals belong on Olympus. She belongs here."

June faltered then, stepping back and turning to Henry. She looked at him, tears threatening to spill over, and he squeezed her arm reassuringly. When he gave her the barest hint of a nod, she spun back to Zeus. "Take us home. Now. We will raise Evelyn there just fine on our own."

Hera raised a finger. "Just to be clear, she will not have the protection that you did. It has been expressly forbidden for any god, or titan, to become companion to man again." She looked pointedly at Typhon, who was staring at his feet.

It dawned on June then. That's why he hadn't been around. He wasn't allowed to. She really thought he'd come back with them . . .

She straightened her shoulders and snapped at Zeus. "Never mind that. I stand by what I said."

She felt Henry move closer behind her and turned to see him nod his head firmly.

Zeus sighed and waved his hand. "Very well."

The world around June's little family dissolved.

Acknowledgements

Thank you to Pierce, for being so patient with me while I spent countless nights spacing out in front of my computer, trying to finish this book. And for the awesome dinners you made throughout! I know this isn't really your style, but I hope you enjoy it anyway. Your endless support is the best gift I could ever ask for.

A very important thank you goes to Sarah as well. Our Thursday night get-togethers and your progressive beta read of this book helped me get through it so much easier than if I'd been on my own in June's world. I promise I'll give your inspired character a bit more action in the next book.

Massive thanks R. W. Harrison, author of The Onyx Trilogy, and my very first friend in the wide world of writing. Your input after the first draft helped so much more than you'll probably ever know, and I hope you enjoy what this evolved into. We may write in very different genres, but you've always got a supporter in me.

To my entire publication team – but especially my editor, Darcy, this book would be a hot mess without you. Thank you for believing in the story, getting it print ready, and agreeing to stick around for the rest of the series. My assistant, Sara, for keeping me organised and being the woman behind the curtain and picking up my breadcrumbs. And my beta and ARC team – Christyn, Cheyanna, Nicole, Jonnah, Lizelle, and all sixty others – Your feedback helped this story come to life! The Myth of June would not have made it any further than my work in progress file without you.

To Aamna, Kimberly, Matt, Niel, and the countless others who helped out with this book from conception to print. You all did amazing work with the covers, edits, art, and all the things in between.

To my daughter. You're too young to know this now, but you inspire me daily, and I write for you. I hope you understand that you really can do anything.

Last, but certainly not least, thank you, Reader, for giving my work a shot. I hope you enjoyed the story, and I hope you're ready for more. I look forward to seeing you in my next book shortly.

About the Author

Ariana Daniels-Annachi is an accountant and artist originally from The United States. She now lives in Australia with her daughter, after having a memoir published in 2020, followed by a childrens book, she quickly decided to dive into fiction. She now spends her time writing and painting, outside of designing jewellery and working in a small shop. Follow her on instagram, facebook, or tiktok @abdanielsannachi. To learn more about her and her upcoming books, visit:

www.abdanielsannachi.com

CPSIA information can be obtained
at www.ICGtesting.com
Printed in the USA
LVHW032313070722
722990LV00001B/76